# THE
# GARGOYLE
# DILEMMA

## *The Enchanted Rock Immortals* World
### Releases by Author

**Eve Cole**
Avian
The Dragon's Phoenix
Alpha
Anomaly
The Mate Maker

**Fenley Grant**
Sorcery, Snakes, and Scorpions: A Love Story
Witches, Werewolves, and War: A Love Story
Unwed, Unfed, and the Undead: A Love Story
Curses, Cats, and Crime: A Love Story
Potions, Pinwheels, and Possibilities: A Love Story

**Robin Lynn**
Of Magic, Love, and Fangs
The Demon King's Runaway Bride

**Susan Person**
Fae Undone
Fae Redone

**Amanda Reid**
The Wolf Shifter's Redemption
The Demon's Shifter Mate
The Fae's Obsession
The Shifter's Savior
The Lion Shifter's Trust

**Sharla Wylde**
A Mermaid's Quest

THE

# GARGOYLE
# DILEMMA

AN ENCHANTED ROCK IMMORTALS NOVELLA

# AMANDA
# REID

ISBN: 978-1-951770-14-3

*For my Family.*
*Be you part of the one I was born to, the one I married into, or the one I gathered throughout my life, your love and support are so treasured.*

# THE ENCHANTED ROCK IMMORTALS

**Demons and Vampires. Elves and Fairies. Mages and Witches. Werewolves and Dragons. Psychics and Telekinetics.**

These magical beings and more exist, rubbing shoulders in their daily lives with unsuspecting humans. But a supernatural society doesn't happen without order. Millennia ago, the Clans —Sanguis, Fae, Magic, Shifter, and Human Paranormal— wisely formed a Council to maintain that order. The end? To ensure the worlds of human and paranormal beings didn't collide and break out into a war that would result in the extermination or subjugation of either.

As human civilization progressed, the first council formed the All Clan Charter at the natural vortex in Great Zimbabwe, giving each clan a voice in the administration of affairs both between the clans and with humans. Next, Asia formed its council at Chengtu Vortex. Then European at Warel Chakra Vortex. North America came next at the natural vortex humans called Enchanted Rock, in what today is known as Texas.

Now, thriving communities of paranormal beings exist in

and around the granite outcropping. Humans scrabble over the dome, not suspecting an entire city exists within its confines: the North American Council and all its departments —Legislative, Administrative, Security, Medical, Vortex Transportation, and Legal, plus restaurants, clan hotels, and shops catering to the paranormal crowds.

Also under that dome? Intrigue, politics, and most importantly, love.

These are the stories of The Enchanted Rock Immortals.

# CHAPTER 1

Cher Velasco hit the push bar on the coffee shop's door and walked into the New Mexico morning with its endless, crisp blue sky. She inhaled, glorying in the way the frigid air seized her lungs.

The sensation reminded her of her childhood, waiting for the school bus, huddled with two other children on the dirt road near the tattered mailbox row. She chuckled as she made her way around the converted house situated on her home town's main thoroughfare, a narrow state highway piled three feet high on either side with plowed snow.

If you'd told her she'd long for those raw days before she left Chama and her grandmother, the only family she had left, she'd have called you a liar. But Central Texas had a way of evaporating people's daydreams about never being cold again, vaporizing them like a shallow puddle on a sunny August afternoon. Best enjoy the beautiful weather now. Inbound storms threatened to bring in up to five feet of snow over the next couple of days.

Skirting an icy patch on the narrow sidewalk, she headed

toward the parking lot behind the building. She opened her SUV's door, climbed onto the running board, leaned way forward, and tucked her giant paper coffee cup into the console's holder. Thank goodness for Mountain Perk. Her grandmother's coffee, made from instant crystals, was abysmal. Cher didn't want to offend the woman who raised her, but the second word in the term 'instant coffee' should be stricken from every language on Earth.

Her senses sparked, shooting fiery embers to her belly, and she paused with one booted foot in the floorboard preparing to climb into the driver's seat. What was this? She wasn't reviewing case investigation facts, nor was she even on the job for that matter. Perhaps she'd confused the sensation for indigestion caused by the second cup of strong coffee.

With a rub across her stomach over the belted puffy jacket, she dismissed the sparks. The burning tingles increased.

No mistaking them now.

A car door's slam caught her attention, and she glanced over her shoulder. A tall man wearing a thin, gray wool jacket strode away from a relatively new, yet unremarkable, gray Subaru parked on the small gravel parking lot's far side. *Him?* A halo of faint sparkles glittered around the figure.

Surprise had her momentarily rooted to the spot. Sentences in her reports or numbers on spreadsheets got this treatment, but never before with people.

*Focus—he's a clue.*

The small screaming voice in her head broke through her stupor. In a flash, she took in his form, her mind's eye storing snapshots. A dark gray, wool ball cap covered thick dark hair which curled at his nape. He'd pulled the brim low, and with the heavy cloud-cover, the shadow revealed little—a strong jaw, a slight dimple on his chin, and scowling lips. Broad shoulders hunched against the cold. Flat torso. Jeans clad his long legs, the fabric molded to heavy thighs, and he'd shoved his hands deep in the pockets. New gray and black hiking boots exhibited little wear.

The images plugged into her memory banks like bits of data into a computer. Nothing seemed to connect.If only she could see his face. She flicked a glance back to the man who'd stepped onto the sidewalk close to the coffee shop's building.

*Look at me.* If she were a telepath, she could possibly read his mind or compel him with a mental command. But no. She only had the meager psychic ability to sense patterns and clues to investigations.

Should she follow him into the coffee shop? Probably not. After all, she was only an analyst, not an agent, and certainly had no arrest powers. Or weapons with her if he were dangerous. Maybe she could just view his face...

*Look at me.*

He lifted his head from studying the ground where he walked, and glanced over his shoulder.

Cher froze as she took in his features. A slight scruff hedged the planes of his cheeks and jaw. Chiseled nose. High cheekbones. The new images fed into her memory.

When her gaze collided with his hard stare, her breath caught. She found it impossible to tear her attention away from his steely eyes fringed with impossibly dark, sinfully thick lashes under a slash of black brows. Far beyond handsome, he ventured into sexiest-man-of-the-year territory.

His stride paused, his eyes widened, then his brows slammed together with his lips compressing. He understood he'd drawn her attention, and she'd marked him as a paranormal.

For some weird reason, the scowl didn't intimidate her. She shot him a smirk and waved.

Along with his glare, he lifted his upper lip to reveal a sharpened incisor before he turned away.

Once again, the warning inexplicably triggered her amusement not fear. While she tracked him around the corner to the street, she added together the clues.

Starting with the fact she investigated paranormal crimes for the North American Council Security at Enchanted Rock, he was connected to the paranormal world. Add to the list were his height, somewhere six-feet six, the relatively light coat when everyone else wore heavy, insulating layers for January in Northern New Mexico—beanies, down parkas, heavy snow boots—while he wore an open neck on his flannel shirt and no scarf. Plus, his broad, rock-hard physique, facial features, eyes…fangs.

They all added up to gargoyle.

Gargoyle? She didn't have any suspects who were…wait. Terri Porter's half-brother was a gargoyle. She was wanted for a felony. Terri had skipped town, and Cher hadn't been able to ferret out any new patterns or locations where she might be found. Even her brother had disappeared… Cher dredged her memory banks for the report she'd compiled more than six months ago.

Ethan Porter.

*Gotcha.* Satisfaction surged in her blood. He'd gone to ground at roughly the same time. Cher compared her moments-ago mental snapshot to the photo she'd found on his business' website.

She inhaled sharply as the confirmation settled.

Ethan Porter had just walked by her.

Then the confirmation smacked her upside the head.

Holy shit. *Ethan-freaking-Porter* just walked by her. *Hmm...* According to Cher's report, he didn't have a rep for violence.

Maybe she could learn more about him, including where he was staying or heading.

She shut the SUV's door and started down the walkway after the male NAC Security needed to interview either as a witness or potential suspect for aiding and abetting his sister. Terri Porter had sold out an NACS colleague's secret and rare ability to over twenty crime syndicates then pocketed the money. The betrayal of proprietary NACS information? A felony and twenty years in jail. It wouldn't be so bad for Terri if she'd only betrayed NACS, but she'd taken every dirty dollar from every offer after advertising the information would go only to the highest bidder. If the woman had been a less annoying and self-centered, Cher might've summoned a shred of sympathy. Now, Terri had not only NACS investigators hunting to bring her to justice, but the woman also faced an army of paranormal mob assassins bent on revenge.

Intent on following the gargoyle, Cher paid little attention to her footing and slid on the icy patch. Her screech cut off when she landed on her tailbone.

White flashes popped in her vision while the pain radiated up her spine. Several breaths later, she pushed to her feet and rubbed her offended posterior. She pressed past her pulsing tailbone and hobble-jogged the twenty or so steps to the corner.

Huh. Not on the main street. Maybe he went into Mountain Perk. A quick scan through the bay window of the converted bungalow said no Porter.

Dammit, where—

The start of a car's engine sounded from behind her.

He must've doubled back through the side yard of the next house. She sprinted awkwardly, retracing her steps to the parking lot just in time to catch a glimpse of the Subaru's tail

lights speeding down the alley. She ignored her throbbing tailbone and raced through the gravel and frozen mud. She might
be able to catch the license plate.

At the narrow passage's edge, she skidded to a stop. The
small, sport SUV had already rounded the corner and headed
back to the main street. She spun and headed to the highway,
careful to avoid the icy patch on the sidewalk. While she ran,
no gray Subaru passed on the road ahead, and her hopes
plummeted.

She turned her focus north at the front walk lining the
highway.

In the distance, the Subaru sped up Highway 17 toward
the Colorado border, a mere seven miles away. She'd probably
scared him off. With her hands on her hips, she glanced back
at her SUV. A little knot formed in her belly. If she had
jumped in her vehicle first, she might've followed him a little to
see where he went.

Bad idea. Shadowing him into a coffee shop was one thing,
but vehicle surveillance was a completely different animal.
Though he had no rap sheet for violence, assuming he was
with his sister, he was protecting her and might get desperate
should he think she tailed him. But if she had merely stayed
with her SUV after she recognized him, she could've at least
recorded the license plate.

She shook her head at her temporary lapse in logic. The
gargoyle's sexiness must've rattled her. Weird. She'd never
found a suspect attractive before. What would her best friend,
Ro Nlongo, a full-fledged NACS agent, think of her now?

Cher rolled her eyes at her stupidity. Ro would say field
work wasn't Cher's job, and she should stick to being an intel
analyst.Ro would also say Cher should get laid if she was
thinking a suspect 'hawt.'

She snorted a soft, self-deprecating laugh at her raging

libido, then shook off the idea she should've done more. If she called in the information to the intelligence desk, NACS could catch up with the Porters.

Time with her ailing grandma was more important right now.

# CHAPTER 2

E than Porter slammed the cabin's door shut, his mood more foul than an injured dragon.

All he wanted was a damn espresso and to pick up some real coffee, not the standard brands the tiny town's equally tiny grocery store supplied. He pulled off his jacket, threw it on the hook in the minuscule mudroom, crossed through the compact kitchen, then sank into a simple upholstered side chair. Frustration ate at his temples, and he massaged his forehead.

Had that woman recognized him? She certainly knew he wasn't human. She sure wasn't intimidated by his menacing glare and hint of fang warning her to back off. The cheeky little wave stuck in his mind, as did the obvious female appreciation in her amber-eyed stare.

But who was she? Definitely too short for a fae, except maybe gremlin or an exceptionally tall dwarf at maybe five feet. Nah. Too cute for a gremlin, and if a dwarf, she wouldn't be able to stand the morning's sunny skies without eye protection. Didn't fit for Clan Sanguis—her petite, curvy body, visible even under her down coat, didn't say lean, rangy demon. And they preferred a phenotype to turn into a vampire, someone who matched their lithe physical standards. The lush chestnut curls rolling out from under her knit cap begged him to tug on the springs. Maybe a shifter with all that glorious hair, though he again struggled to find one species of their clan who was that diminutive and shapely. Which said probably either Clan Magic or Clan Human Paranormal.

He pictured her lips curled into a sly grin, her perky little nose wrinkled with her amusement at his threat. Her—

*Stop.* Didn't matter what she looked like. Or even what clan she belonged to. She had recognized him as another paranormal being. And the simple fact stung because it meant they'd have to move again.

A frustrated grumble escaped his throat with the impossible situation. He tipped his head back to searched the planks and beams lining the ceiling as if they would hold the answer to whether he and his sister should relocate.

The solution shone as clearly as a fae fyre crystal's flash. Dammit. Six months remained on the lease. Finding another one in the middle of nowhere who accepted cash, didn't ask a lot of questions, and provided a clean, habitable, if dated, home wasn't easy.

Sure, Terri rescued him from the Sunda Komodo shifter crime family by paying off his father's debts. All she'd accomplished by her little stunt was land herself in boiling water and expand his pursuers as a target to bring her out into the open. He loved his sister, but damn, her impulsiveness did nothing to improve his situation. From threatened by one crime family to threatened by almost twenty hadn't helped one bit.

Though he wanted to do nothing but shuck his clothes and take to the skies for the next decade, he'd given his promise to his father to take care of Terri. Gargoyles, unlike most dark fae, kept their word once given. Luckily for the rest of the fae clan—elves, gremlins, sprites, and the like—when they broke their vow, they didn't experience physical torture. He rubbed a hand over his face. If he hadn't been able to raise the capital to pay off the Komodo syndicate for his father's debts, where would he get the money to pay the myriad of people Terri had shafted?

He tabled the too-familiar conundrum in favor of the now.

Though he really wanted to just end the flight and turn himself and Terri in, she'd never agree, and the act certainly wouldn't satisfy his vow. How could he protect her in jail? While exceptionally secure, inmates died from violence on occasion in the North American Council's prison. The convicts would surely find out Terri had a price on her head.

Running remained his only answer, at least for the present.

He glanced around the compact cabin's spare living space which bore none of his own personal items. All of his possessions could be packed in less than an hour because everything had to fit in the back of the Subaru. Plus, there hadn't been time to bring much more than a suitcase after he learned what his sister had done. Well, half-sister, but sister nonetheless.

"Did you get the coffee?" Terri asked from over his shoulder.

He didn't turn, but focused on a faded autumn landscape hanging on the wall next to the pot-belly stove's chimney. Could she leave today? No way. Her belongings took up the remaining space in the car, including the back seat. "No coffee. Another paranormal recognized me, maybe not my face, but she knew I was paranormal. We can't risk it. You need to gather your things. We'll leave in the morning."

A petulant huff sounded over his shoulder and her hard heels fell on the rough wooden floor. Terri came to stand before him with her hands on her cocked hips. "Why do we have to leave? I like it way better here than the last place." She grimaced with a delicate shudder. "That place was gross and smelled like mouse pee. And this landlady is so nice."

Though she was half-gargoyle, her other half was human. Sometimes the fae genes broke through but not with Terri. If she were full gargoyle, she'd have the ability to shift into a being with wings, fangs, supernatural strength, and nearly impenetrable skin. As it stood, her sole paranormal gift was a weak ability to read minds. Since most in his world learned to guard their thoughts, her psychic skill worked mainly against regular humans.

He shouldn't have to review with her how a single gargoyle wouldn't be able to stop the hordes of beings chasing after them, let alone keep her from NAC prison for stealing and selling restricted information. He shouldn't have to remind her, so he wouldn't.

"You thought this place was gross just a month ago." He planted his hands on the chair's worn, oak-plank armrests and pushed to standing, forcing her to step back.

Her clear gray eyes widened, and one of her hands rose to fiddle with a curl of her dark ponytail, which she'd artfully brought forward over her shoulder.

Wait a minute. He took in her form. Full makeup, which she never bothered applying if staying in the cabin. Hair styled. Tight jeans under her pretty plaid shirt which matched her eyes. He snorted a disbelieving laugh. "I thought you were going to the grocery store. Who are you meeting?"

Fleeting surprise lifted her brows before she smoothed her features and dropped her hand to join the other behind her back. "Meeting someone? Who would I meet here?"

Fury slammed through him with her obvious lie, and he flexed his hands before shoving them in his pockets. Sometimes he just wanted to shake some sense into her. Her selfish party life was over, though she didn't want to acknowledge the fact. Witness her wanting to mingle in town, probably with a man. Especially now that another paranormal had recognized him. Hell, she could be meeting with a bounty hunter and not even know.

Several slow breaths through his nose later, he could finally address her question. "Doesn't matter who. Be ready for me to load the car tonight. We'll leave by six tomorrow."

With those words, he turned and started for the front door. He must escape for just a bit to cool his temper. Gargoyles were notoriously hot-headed, though his friends often called him 'Iceman' for his legendary calm and logic. The nickname didn't hold around his family. For some reason, the ones he loved had a way of unleashing all the emotions he kept under wraps.

"I can't possibly be ready by tonight." Terri's voice had reverted to her teen whine. When he didn't respond to her statement, she asked, "Where are you going?"

He paused with his hand on the doorknob. "I have to go notify Ms. Two-Birds. Maybe I can sweet talk her into returning the two-month's penalty for breaking the rental contract early."

"You're serious?"

He didn't respond verbally to her screech, letting his 'what-do-you-think?' stare speak instead. When her pink-glossed lips hung open with shock, he yanked open the door.

"But, we can't leave tomorrow because—"

The door's slam cut off any ridiculous justification she might've offered for staying.

Getting to his landlady's house required a bit of driving, despite the two houses being on the same property. The cabin stood in one corner at a much higher elevation, while the ranch house sat a couple thousand acres away in a little valley on the opposite side of the tract. A rambling livestock trail would take him there, but he wasn't in the mood for the two-hours' walk, though the trek would allow him more time to calm down and think.

Not think about whether he made the right decision. He and his sister couldn't afford recognition. A friend told him there was a one-thousand-fae-gold-piece bounty on Terri's head from feared gangster Griffith Jenkins alone. The amount still clogged Ethan's throat with terror for his sister. There could be dozens of bounty hunters searching for her by now if the other crime families she'd conned took the same tack.

The cute little paranormal could've been one of those bounty hunters.

Hopefully, he'd thrown her off-track. When he'd left Chama, he chose to go north and used the last street he could to double back through the other side of town. Then he went west on the highway toward Pagosa Springs and back to the cabin. He pressed his foot to the accelerator and his practical sport SUV leapt forward, bouncing up the mile-long, packed dirt path to the highway. His mind raced, trying to figure out where to relocate. Montana? Too many people. Alaska? Would there be enough isolated housing available? Canada maybe?

Regardless, he'd have to find a job soon. He'd been unprepared when NACS froze his bank account, and he'd fled with what he had in his safe. Not enough for long-term life on the run. The cash he wasted on this cabin and its two-month's rent proviso for breaking the lease was a budgetary hit he couldn't afford. Some rapid calculation as he bumped along said he had enough for the upfront cost of another lease, but no more. And he couldn't afford Terri's exposure by her finding employment, especially when she was so indiscrete.

Then there was the tricky issue of the signed contract. His word would be broken. If he could get Ms. Two-Bird's to release him, even if verbally, he could avoid the consequences bequeathed only to gargoyles.

Finally, he turned onto his landlady's lane, which was wider and smoother than the cabin's. After he parked, he sucked in a breath. He really would hate leaving here. He enjoyed the solitude at the foot of the Rocky Mountains. The granite sung in time with his soul as he cruised the blessedly cool nights, soaring amongst the clouds, sweeping down to the lodgepole pines, surveying the moonlit valleys from a perch high on a boulder outcropping.

He shook himself. This was just a place. He and Terri could find another.

Once he'd parked, he exited and made his way under a broad porch to the front door. He might've called, but mobile reception sucked this far from Chama.

He pushed the intercom button which served as a doorbell. "Ms. Two-Birds, it's Ethan." He released the button. In retrospect, he shouldn't have used their real first names. Not that he had any prior experience hiding identities.

"Come on in. I'm in the kitchen." The elderly woman's warbly voice emerged tinny and flat through the speaker. A buzz and click came as her offer ended.

He stifled his residual annoyance, attempted to smooth the frown gathered between his brows, then pushed open the modest ranch-styled house's thick, oak front door and entered the shadowed hall. Following the taste bud-triggering scent of spiced meat, he paced by the living room on his left and traversed the short passage toward the bright light.

When he rounded the corner, he found his landlady at the range. Wearing a fluffy purple cardigan around her thin shoulders, she stood between her walker's rails while she stirred a pot of what smelled like chili. The smile she greeted him with carried the sun's warmth and pushed up her apple cheeks until the corners of her eyes crinkled. "To what do I owe this pleasure?"

He waited until she'd put the lid back on the pot and oriented herself with her walking aid. "I hate to say that we're going to have to leave. Tomorrow."

Ms. Two-Bird's smile melted away, replaced by a look of concern. She reached across the narrow kitchen island which separated them and placed her hand on his. "I'm so sorry. What's happened? You and your wife seemed to like the cabin so much."

His palm began to sweat under her kind touch. He suppressed the need to withdraw from her hand while he cursed himself for not finding a better excuse while he drove over. "Uh...A family emergency. My...uncle died."

The concern lighting her eyes through her owlish glasses' thick lenses shamed him. He may not go back on his word, but of late, lying had become a necessity, and he hated every fraudulent word dropping from his lips. Especially when it was to this woman who fairly glowed with kindness.

"Of course you must go. I'm going to miss you around here. You've been so helpful, I'll only take one month's rent instead of two for breaking the lease. Are you sure you're going to leave tomorrow—"

"Someone's coming up your driveway." His enhanced hearing had picked up the rumble of an engine, a truck he'd guessed. The relief of being released from his word fled and his shoulders tensed. If bounty hunters had found him and Terri, he couldn't risk this lovely woman's life.

"That would be my granddaughter. She came in from Texas to spend some time with me. She was picking up some groceries for me in Chama. Come, I want you to meet her."

Ms. Two-Birds leaned on her walker and shuffled toward the front of the house.

Ethan followed, watching his landlady carefully as her thick white braid swayed against her cardigan. A normal human shouldn't recognize him. Though he'd rather not spread his face around more than he had to, he didn't have the heart to deny the old woman. How could he after she'd pressed a delicious green chili enchilada casserole into his hands for the first night at the cabin.

The front door opened, revealing a woman laden with plastic grocery bags.

He froze.

The same woman from the coffee shop's parking lot.

# CHAPTER 3

Laden with all the groceries she'd picked up on her trip to town, Cher huffed a bit as she shouldered through her grandma's front door.

From the corner of her eye, she spied the yellow tennis balls which capped the non-wheeled ends of her grandma's walker. When Cher lifted her head, she froze. A dark form hovered like death's shadow over her hunched abuela.

A scream clogged her throat, but it couldn't escape because she couldn't get her lungs to work.

"Cher, I'm so glad you're home." Grandma's voice held no fear of the apparition in the dark hallway.

Cher swallowed her terror and focused on the figure. Not a shadow. A man. Her lungs decided to work again, and she released her breath in a rush. Just a man. "Grandma, you really need to put some lights on." She heaved one heavily-laden hand to the switch and flipped on the hallway light, then turned back, taking in exactly who stood behind her beloved grandma.

Only to freeze again.

*It's him.*

The same gargoyle from the parking lot. Ethan Porter. Fear surged again. Had he come to kill her? She couldn't discount the idea he'd figured out her identity and came to warn her not to say anything. A gargoyle could rip her fragile grandmother in half with a bare finger's flick. Apprehension slithered its slimy way down her spine. Too late for his warning. She'd already called NACS.

"Cher, you and Ethan have met?"

Her grandmother's voice tugged her focus away from the witness-slash-possible suspect and the threat he posed. "Why would you think we've met?"

"I thought you said 'It's him.'"

Cher's cheeks heated. "Uh, no. I said…uh…I'm warm."

Her grandma's puzzled expression made Cher's cheeks blaze even more. She gestured with the bags, hoping to divert attention from the subject. "Hey, these are a bit heavy. Can I get them to the kitchen?"

"Of course." Her grandmother made the awkward turn with her walker in the narrow space.

Though he stared at the front door, Porter turned and led the small train back to the kitchen. He rounded the island to the far side. Would he make a run out the back?

Like she could stop him. Her main priority now became ensuring he didn't hurt her grandmother. All Cher had as a defense was the spelled fae silver blade in her purse slung over her shoulder. With clatters and thunks, she dropped the grocery bags on the counter.

A can broke free from one of the thin, plastic bags and rolled toward Porter. He easily caught the tin of beans before it hit the floor.

Cher used the distraction to quickly slip her hand into her purse and palm the blade, inching the grip up into her sleeve. The knife would be the only thing she could use against gargoyle skin. Though they appeared human, their hide could withstand fifty-caliber rounds. One of the vulnerable spots in their human forms were their eyes, but those were too small a target. She'd purchased the knife for a time she never knew would come. The spells embedded in the silver were guaranteed to be effective on every known being. With the self-defense training she'd religiously maintained over the years, she just might be able to get her grandmother to the safe room if he became violent.

Porter carefully placed the can in front of Cher, and she tensed for an attack. A small, ironic smile hovered at his lips, as if he knew she'd just palmed her knife and planned to fight back.

He withdrew his hand, and shifted his gaze to her grandmother. "Well, Ms. Two-Birds, I need to be getting back." His tone was stiff and formal and very rushed. "Thank you for the cabin."

Confused, she turned to her grandmother. "Cabin?"

"Ethan and his wife rented Coot's old place for six months, but they had a family emergency and have to leave."

"Wife?" She swiveled her gaze to him and to the spot where his left hand rested on the counter. He didn't wear a ring. Then again, a lot of men didn't. Nothing in his background indicated a relationship. But sometimes, some *very* rare times, she didn't uncover a bit of data.

"Yes." If possible, his tone had hardened to granite.

She'd bet her next paycheck he'd presented his sister as his wife.

"Terri, isn't it?" Grandma started to take groceries from their bags and set them on the counter.

*Holy shit.* Though Cher had expected the answer, energy began to bounce through her. She glanced at the phone on the side table beyond Porter, conflicted. She both didn't want him to leave so NACS could come and scoop him up, and also needed him to leave now because of her vulnerable grandma.

A mask of calm slipped over his face. She wouldn't have known his expression to be bogus if not for the fleeting, wide-eyed shock which he'd covered. "Why, yes." He shoved his hands into his front pockets. "Well, I need to get back to pack so we can leave in the morning. I'll leave the key under the front door's mat."

Cher laughed. "You can't leave—" She caught herself before she revealed there was a huge blizzard forecasted overnight. The road to the highway may not be passable for the next week, which is why she'd gone to town to pick up extra supplies. Meanwhile, Cher could call headquarters again and report he hadn't actually left town and Terri Porter was with him. There might be time for agents to get to Chama before the two could pull a disappearing act again.

"Why can't I leave?" His tone slid low, holding a bit of a growl.

"Because…because…" Panic slammed through her, her pulse jumping to a gallop. What excuse could she use?

Her grandma paused in her unloading of a bag of canned products. "Cher?"

She spied the Dutch oven containing chili on the stove. Bingo. "I'm sure Grandma would want you two to have some of her chili for your last dinner." Would he buy the lame reason? She held her breath. If he didn't, would he use violence to make her talk? Violence against her grandmother even?

"Wonderful idea," Grandma said, her tone bright with delight. "I should've thought of it."

Porter pulled his hands from the counter and held them up as if to hold off a charging minotaur. "No, really, I couldn't inconvenience you."

"If you're packing, you won't have time to make dinner. I insist." Grandma turned to the stove. "Mija, could you get something to put it in?"

Since he didn't appear to be aggressive, merely wanting to get out of the house, Cher's muscles began to relax, though she still kept her knife's sheath tucked in her sweater's sleeve. She pivoted, opened the pantry, and located a medium-sized plastic container longer than it was tall. She set it next to the stove where her grandmother held a ladle ready. The whole time, Cher had tracked the male in her peripheral vision. She could almost feel the waves of impatience...or was it desperation...emanating from him.

"Don't worry, we'll be done in no time. I'm sure you want to get back to your wife and get ready to leave." She forced a reassuring smile with her words. Prevarication, lies, fibs, whatever someone called untruths, Cher hated them. But she'd do it to buy the agents time.

That he'd shifted toward the end of the island, closer to the exit, hadn't escaped Cher's notice. Hopefully, she hadn't spooked him so much he'd make a run for it tonight.

A *snap-snap* signaled her grandma finished securing the top.

Relieved, Cher picked up the container with her empty hand. Warmth seeped through her fleece-lined glove.

"I can take that," he offered, reaching to take the chili from her.

"Oh no." She pulled the chili to the side. "You don't have gloves on, and this is really hot. I'll just walk it to your car for you. I'm sure It'll be cool enough to handle when you get to the cabin."

So solicitous. But she wanted his tag number. She'd been distracted by the clouds beginning to pile on the horizon when she drove up to the house and hadn't paid attention to the car. A ranch hand's wife had one similar, and her lapsed attention made her forget they were rarely up here this time of year with the large animals at lower altitudes.

Porter didn't protest her offer, merely nodded his assent. He said good-bye to her grandmother, then followed Cher outside.

She carefully placed the container on his front seat's floorboard. While a quick scan revealed nothing she could use to identify that for sure Terri Porter stayed with him, Cher didn't believe in coincidences. She was certain this man was Ethan Porter and his 'wife's' name just solidified the idea in her mind.

While she'd placed the chili, he'd slid his massive frame into the driver's seat. "Thanks." A quick grin curved the corner of his lips, bringing his face from broodingly handsome to A-list movie star.

She inhaled sharply as desire shot right to her core, leaving her all tingly and wanting to giggle. Alarmed, she stepped back. "Be careful." She suppressed a wince at her words, which were the only thing she could think to say. No one had affected her this way before. With one grin, he'd gone from handsome to panty-wetting. That he was a suspect confused her even further. She knew better. Suspects, felons, anyone on that side of her job remained off-limits.

He started the car, reversed, and trundled down the drive to the county road leading to the highway.

She tracked him carefully, committing the license plate to memory. If he were smart, he would change it. Maybe he wasn't smart. Then again, the way his gaze took in everything indicated he paid attention to detail. She shivered at the memory of his stormy, dark blue eyes, then shoved away the idea she'd be attracted to him.

He was firmly in the suspect category now that she'd discovered him harboring his sister.

Cher had another call to make.

# CHAPTER 4

E than stared through the cabin's window, which wind-blown snow had half-obscured over the last two days. After leaving Ms. Two-Bird's house, he'd returned to find Terri had only begun packing. At the time, the clock had said half-past three. Of course she wouldn't be ready in time with clothes strewn all over her small room and her five suitcases still largely empty. Even if she worked all night, there could've been no way for her to be ready. Hadn't mattered. By morning, the snow had already been too deep, with forecasts predicting blizzard conditions. He suspected she slacked in her packing to teach him a lesson for slamming out of the cabin.

At least the snow had stopped. While the storm's tempest had stacked a drift against the cabin on the west face, the actual depth achieved only about three and a half feet.

Only. Only deep enough to make leaving an impossibility. *He* could escape if he wanted—cold and piles of snow didn't affect him and his wings. But the blizzard with the strong winds would make taking Terri unfeasible. If he had to fight off killers, too, he might drop her. Plus, if he carried her, he couldn't pack any but the most basic possessions.

Then again, the snow piled deep enough to make it prob-
able that no one would be able to get in, either, including
bounty hunters. Unless they had wings too.

He'd have to dust the blizzard's output from the satellite
dish again, which was the only way to receive Wi-Fi. He'd
already braved the blinding snow twice. It would be good to
get a weather report. Plus, he needed to find someone with a
plow. He turned from the glass with its edges of beautiful,
geometrically patterned frost glinting in the mid-day, cloud-
obscured sunlight. The itch to escape the cabin and soar high
enough to take in the pristine beauty hit him hard and
tunneled under his skin. *Tonight, if the weather holds.*

"I tried to tell you we couldn't go, but you didn't want to
listen." Terri put a bowl of soup in the microwave. Luckily, the
power hadn't gone out yet.

Terri's tone had regained the sullen-teen shades he loved so
much. His pleasant thoughts of exploring snow-covered peaks
plummeted, replaced by simmering resentment. He caught
himself as his father's final gritty words rang in his ears,
'Promise to take care of your sister.'

Plus, she was right. He'd slammed the door on her. Even
the tiny female, Cher, had been right, for that was surely what
she meant when she cut off her words two days ago. He'd
been mulling over the entire encounter with the sexy lady. If
he hadn't been checking out her sparkling hazel eyes and her
kissable lips, he would've caught on that her chili offer had
been a blatant cover up for a slip about the weather.

The obvious conclusion? She knew his identity and wanted
him to stay here. The why escaped him. But it couldn't be
good.

And as sure as the Unseelie made gargoyles, she'd palmed
a fae silver blade in that kitchen, right in front of her grandmother. He'd scented the peculiar tang of the metal mixed

with the Penetrate spell's ozone and licorice. In the closer confines of the room, he'd also been able to sniff out her clan, Human Paranormal, along with her particular enticing aroma of rich coffee, spice, and rosemary.

He couldn't be sure if she retrieved the knife for protection or attack. The former, most likely. If she were a bounty hunter, she'd had plenty of opportunities to strike him on the way to the car. That led to another question. If not out to bag and tag him for money, why would she know who he was at all? He wracked his memories for a meeting, however incidental. Nothing. He knew all of his employees. Ethan worked awful hours to try to salvage the company his father had run into the ground, only to discover Dad had brought in the Sunda mob family for a loan-shark 'rescue.' Ethan had no love life, let alone a social life, at all while he tried to work his way out of the financial hole his father excavated.

He'd reviewed far more than those topics over the last two days. The sweet curve of the woman's hips under the nipped-in waist of her belted down jacket, the rosy curve of her cheek, the springy curls, and the transformative hazel eyes all too often fell into his memory.

"Ethan!"

Fingers snapped in front of his face. Startled, he took a step back.

Terri stood with her hands on her hips. "Have you heard a word I said?" She didn't wait for him to answer. "No, you haven't. We're almost out of food. Six cans of soup. Half a loaf of bread and some peanut butter. If you had let me go to the store like I wanted to two days ago—"

"I'll hunt for game tonight if I have to. I'm going to clear the snow from the satellite dish." Rather than get into an argument she was obviously spoiling for, he reined in his irritation and chose the diplomat's way out.

Leave.

With his last word, he closed the door and waded into the pile of snow on the front stoop, which was on the south side of the small log structure. Since gargoyles were impervious to cold, he didn't bother with a jacket, and he slogged down the steps into the waist-deep drifts. He could cut a path through with a shovel, but his paranormal strength, easily ten times that of a human man, made the going easy. Besides, he only went about a dozen steps.

He crouched and sprung, landing feet first on the roof. He'd chosen the corner where it covered the stoop, so the four-by-four underneath would give more support. Gargoyles also weighed about half as much again as a regular human the same size, and he didn't want to be charged for replacing the wood beam. He couldn't afford his conscience right now.

Several paces up the steeply sloped roof, he quickly dusted off the dish, and he prepared to descend as he came.

The buzzing whine of a small engine rose to his ears over the silence. He snapped up his head toward the cabin's drive-way. Not coming from that direction. Where... He glanced over his shoulder.

About half a mile away, a snowmobile had emerged from a copse of fir where the trail would've led to Ms. Two-Bird's house. Someone out for a ride? His shoulders tensed, and a pit grew in his stomach. The driver throttled up on a clear path to the cabin.

He narrowed his vision. In an orange, hooded snowsuit, the person could've been anyone, but a corkscrew chocolate-and-caramel curl had escaped the hood.

Cher.

Shit. What other reason could she have to come all this way other than to kill them? Yet, announcing her presence with a loud snowmobile made little sense. He jumped off the roof and slogged back to the front door. He kept his gaze narrowed on her while he brushed off his jeans, then he slipped into the cabin.

Terri sent him a nasty glare from her seat at the table where she ate her lunch, but he had zero time for the surliness. "We have company."

Instantly, the sullen grimace shifted to fear. "Who?"

"A human paranormal woman. The reason behind our need to leave."

He raced up to the loft and grabbed one of his guns, thankful he'd paid the extra money for spelled bullets. Without knowing her particular talent as a human paranormal, he might or might not be able to draw it. Most could read minds. Some were telekinetic. Some could plant suggestions in a person's mind. No telling what this one could do, so best to be prepared. He tugged his flannel shirt over the weapon and went to the door. The engine's whine had ceased when he stepped onto the porch, angling his body to make sure she knew she wouldn't be invited inside.

She stood at the back of the snowmobile, which she'd parked right next to the steps, a couple of feet from the snow-covered lump of his car. His palm itched to grab the pistol burning a hole in his lower back.

She straightened, glanced up, and held a large box in her quilted-mittened hands. The metallic-visored goggles now perched on her head, revealing her pert nose and wary, green-gold gaze. She'd unlatched her neck gaiter and slipped her hood back to reveal a cascade of curls.

With her foot on the second step, she stopped when she spied him standing on the porch. She shifted her gaze away then back to him. A hesitant smile hovered on her generous lips, extra rosy today, probably from the cold as she rode over.

"Oh. Hello. My grandmother wanted to make sure you

two were okay. She was worried you may not have many supplies, since you were going to leave, and she sent me with this." Cher hefted the obviously heavy box. "I was just going to put it on the porch for you so I didn't disturb you and…your wife."

How he hated having to examine each word anyone said. She seemed to be telling the truth. Her scent drifted toward him, and his muscles began to relax. His frustration, both from being unable to escape and being trapped with his sister, should have had him tense. Mystified at how Cher's mere essence could burrow into his being and bring him peace, he started forward.

She met him at the edge of the porch and handed over the supplies. With her arms wrapped around her body, she hovered at the edge, obviously wanting to leave. "There's a King Ranch casserole in there, along with mostly canned stuff, frozen vegetables, eggs, a loaf of bread, and a big beef roast."

"Many thanks to you and your grandmother. She guessed right. We are low on food. Would you like to come in and warm up?" Why in the hell did he make the offer? She could still be a threat.

"No." She'd almost shouted the word, then continued in a more modulated voice, "I really need to get back. Another round of snow's on its way. Here in about an hour. Another two feet they say."

His hopes to get out in the next couple of days evaporated, ramping up his urgency to leave. "When do you think we might be able to get a plow?"

"I called Ernest to see when he might make it to Grandma's and here, and he said he's busy trying to keep the main roads clear. He probably won't be free for another couple of days. Since he contracts with the county, that's his priority."

She offered a tight smile. "The next round should just be overnight and into tomorrow."

Two more days? Somehow, he managed to conceal his annoyed growl at the delay and dipped his head in thanks, while he clutched the box all the harder to resist the temptation to hurl the provisions into the snow.

Her gaze focused on his hands, and her lids widened.

Hell. He relaxed his fingers from where they'd crushed the heavy cardboard.

She took a step backward and down one stair. "Well, I need to go." Two more treads and she'd stepped next to her snowmobile. Her need to leave was palpable.

Had he scared her? Why now of all times? The box crushing?

She'd finished tucking her hair back into her hood and settled her goggles, then fiddled at the handlebars. He spied the old-school, pull cord handle, much like someone would start a push mower. Such a tiny woman for such a powerful machine between her legs.

Images flooded his mind. Images of him being the powerful machine between her legs. Need pulsed in his cock. His surprise allowed the visions free rein before he banished them. After this, he wouldn't see her again.

The idea sent disappointment spiraling through his chest. Stupid dick. He'd only known her for all of five minutes. For the last year, he'd had no time for a love life, and he certainly couldn't take time for this beautiful woman right now.

She grabbed the handle and pulled. A sputtering grind came from the engine. For a moment, she stood stock still, then with hesitancy, she pulled the cord once more, receiving the same result. As if the plastic burned her, she released the handle. She glanced over her shoulder and her jaw firmed.

He followed her gaze. Dark clouds walled on the western horizon over the peaks.

When he re-shifted his focus, she'd turned to look at the way she'd come, and her mouth drew into a thin, determined line.

Dammit. He couldn't let her chance it. She could freeze to death. "Even if you followed the snowmobile's trail, you'll have at least a three-hour walk back to your grandmother's house. You won't make it in time. You can stay with us until we can get out."

She banged on the fiberglass engine housing, then attempted to start the machine again, this time with vigor, but she received the same grinding noise. After a huge breath, she turned to him and started up the stairs. Her demeanor became more of one headed toward a fatal date with the fae Sword of Fallen Souls than of someone saved from a frozen death. "I appreciate your offer. It might be ancient, but we just had the thing serviced. Don't know why it won't start."

Her reluctance confused him. "I'd look at it, but I don't think we have much time before the snow falls."

"Are you a mechanic? I thought—"

He'd graduated with a degree in mechanical and structural engineering. Would she know that? "What'd you think?"

She pushed her hood back and pulled off her goggles. "Nothing...uh...I didn't think you worked with your hands."

She noticed his hands? A small bit of warmth hit him in the solar plexus. "Yeah, well, I tinker with engines sometimes."

Cher stared at him.

He stared back.

For long moments, he held her green-ringed golden gaze, then her lids dropped and she shivered.

The small action brought him back from the depths of imagining how those eyes would look when she climaxed. He'd been blocking her way inside by taking up nearly the entire porch. He hefted the box to carry it with one arm, then swept open the door with the other. "My apologies. Won't you come in?"

Her flattened mouth and locked jaw returned. With a nod, she passed into the cabin.

He set the box on the counter and turned to shut the door when Terri screeched, "Oh, my God. Cher Velasco. Are you here to arrest me?"

# CHAPTER 5

With Terri's panicked shriek from the cabin bedroom's doorway, Cher ceased her thigh-*whooshing* strides. She wanted to beat her head against the counter until it made enough of an impression that she'd never accede to doing something so stupid again. But Grandma insisted that Cher check on the 'nice couple' to make sure they were okay.

She put her hands out at her chest. Arrest her? "Terri, I—"

"You're with North American Council Security?"

Cher whipped around to where Ethan had just placed the box on the ancient countertop. His face turned hard, and a steely glint replaced the appreciative gleam in his eyes, which earlier said he might want to lick her all over.

She swallowed, her stomach cramping. She wished she'd told her grandma the snowmobile wouldn't start, though it had been serviced last week. If she were being honest, Cher didn't want them to starve, either, at least before agents could get to them. "Yes. I'm with NACS, but—"

"Put your hands up." While he spoke, he pulled a large-caliber handgun from his back waistband with a smooth, practiced move and pointed the weapon at her.

Cher's brain ceased all coherent thought when she took in the bore's size, which just seemed to grow bigger the longer she stared. Distantly, the cogs in her mind moved once more, and she slowly raised her hands to shoulder height. More cogs moved until her mind raced, and the portions of the Terri Porter file concerning him came in bursts.

Silence reigned for the moments she took to return her focus to the present. Perhaps both Porters were as shocked as she that he pulled the gun on her. Maybe she could talk him down?

"Ethan." She used the tone she would've used on one of her grandmother's shy horses. "I'm not an agent, and can't arrest her. I do know you have nothing criminal in your background. This will only make the inevitable worse."

His gaze turned resolute. "It may. Take off your snow suit."

Fear formed a hard, heavy fist in her stomach. She'd die of exposure if he turned her out into the impending snow storm without any protection. Possibly, she could disarm him by surprise, but gargoyles were immensely strong, too much for her comparatively-meager human paranormal strength. Her best bet was to comply until she had no other choice, then she might be able to use her spelled blade and the satellite phone.

Since he made the decisions right now, she held a hand to him. "I'm going to have to take off my boots. I need to sit down."

With the curt dip of his chin, she rounded the peninsula and pulled out one of the old dining table's oak chairs, to be able to sit and unlace her heavy snow boot. She ignored Terri and her pale features for now to focus on the real threat, sneaking a peek at the gun as she sat. Trembling fingers made the laces much harder for her to pick apart. Finally, she thunked one heavy boot on the wooden floor and started on the second.

At least his trigger finger was outside the guard, so he had some sort of firearms training. Though not an agent, she'd grown up in the country and learned how to handle a gun. The cardinal rules of weapons safety had been drummed into her head, one of which was never point a pistol at anything you didn't intend to shoot.

Damn. He just might shoot her alright. She pushed that thought to the back since the bore appeared no smaller than before, a seemingly giant black hole promising to end her life if she made the wrong move or said the wrong thing.

She yanked off the second boot, and it thumped on the wooden floor boards.

"Now the suit."

Devoid of emotion, his flat words and dead eyes chilled her. The pit in her stomach doubled in size. With a deep breath, she pushed aside the neck gaiter, then unsnapped the placket down the front, ensuring each of her moves were measured while keeping a covert eye on his index finger. She'd have little warning he'd fire the gun otherwise. The coat's zipper made a dull whir in the silence. She wanted to turn to see what Terri was doing, but Cher hadn't heard movement, and she'd rather face the known threat.

*Keep it slow and steady.* One sleeve, then the other. She unhitched the overalls' straps, then resumed her seat to pull off the pants legs. With her snowsuit removed, she stood and draped the set over the chair mostly pushed under the over-hanging peninsula's counter. She held her breath. Maybe he wouldn't find the knife and satellite phone in the orange puffiness.

"Terri, get the rope in the cabinet above the washer." His eyes hadn't strayed from Cher's. "Turn around."

Shit. He was going to bind her. A boulder dripped into her stomach's yawing pit. She'd have no ability to defend herself or resist him if he dumped her outside. "Only if I have your word neither you nor Terri will turn me out into the cold. Otherwise, I will fight you. I'd rather die by gunshot than freeze to death."

Ethan's lips compressed into a thin, bloodless line. "For the record, I don't want to kill you. I just want to protect my sister. I promise not to force you into the cold if you promise not to resist."

Relief sagged her shoulders. She had his word—the word of a gargoyle—which must be enough. He'd experience extreme physical torture if he broke his oath. She'd already notified NACS, and agents would be here as soon as they could. She wanted to blurt out their impending arrival as a last-ditch effort to avoid the rope, but warning him didn't make sense, so she turned toward the pot-bellied stove and put her hands behind her back.

As she pivoted, she caught sight of Terri. The woman's previously angry mouth was now slack and indecision swam in her gaze.

"Tie her." He still must not trust Cher if he'd ordered his sister to perform the dirty deed so he could keep the gun ready. "And make it good. We can't have her escaping."

Terri's soft hand grasped one of Cher's and tied a knot around her wrist, then the woman began a series of three infinity loops to bind her. From the yanks and pulls, the woman had tied the end of the rope to the other end.

A little satisfaction shot through Cher. Terri didn't know enough not to place the binding over Cher's sweater. She might be able to escape if necessary. After all, she, a human paranormal, wasn't bound to her word.

The squeak of rollers hit her ears. He opened and closed drawers in the kitchen, probably searching for a knife or scissors to cut the binding. The dull ones in the utility drawer would take a while to saw through with Terri's mere HP strength.

But the *sckriiiick-sckriiiick* made short work of the rope. A large, heavy hand grasped her upper arm through her sweater's thick wool.

Ethan yanked her arm and moved her into an empty area between the dining table and the living room's couch. One hand held her, while the other began to search her body, not unkindly, but with efficiency. She gritted her teeth and her muscles snapped tight in anticipation of the coming invasive quests.

He stood behind her, and she couldn't tell if he did so from experience or from a television knowledge of law enforcement procedure. She released a breath when he bypassed her breasts to dip lower. He slid his flat hand down her torso, then around the waistband of her jeans.

Air hitched in her lungs. She'd been given enough rudimentary training on the job to know her crotch would come next. A lot could be hidden both at the apex of the thighs or even inside a being. Not that she had anything. But mobile phones, weapons, charms, potions, even magical creatures had been stowed in either a vagina or rectum. The stories she'd heard from agents started a shudder at the base of her spine which she ruthlessly suppressed.

When he passed over her crotch, she thanked the Source for sparing her the indignity. Being searched by a man who Cher had a hard time banishing from her dreams the last two nights? How embarrassing.

From the corner of her eye, she spotted him crouching down and running his hands over her ankles. The light glinted off his black hair. Ah ha. A television knowledge of procedure then, because even with her hands restrained, she could turn and knee him in the face. She'd probably break her kneecap in the process, so maybe not. She might get him off balance, but where would she go? And where had the gun gone? Was it in his waistband, or did his sister now hold the pistol?

*Stay cool. He said he didn't want to kill you. He promised not to put you into the cold.*

*You can survive this.*

He straightened and to her nose rose his scent, the beautiful aroma of the pine-covered, windswept peaks she climbed as a child. It locked into a part of her being and created a longing spiraling through her. If only she'd met this male in another place and another time, when they could get to know each other irrespective of their worlds.

The idea brought her up short. He was a suspect, a suspect holding her hostage to help his sister. This fact erased her stupid fantasies, and she slowed her breathing. Focus. She must have all of her wits to get out of this. They didn't need to be addled by some gargoyle who smelled addictive and looked as hawt as El Paso in August.

"Terri, check around her breasts and crotch."

Cher tensed. She didn't have anything to hide in either place, but still.

"What?" Terri's screech came from the kitchen.

He hefted a breath and let it go as if asking for patience. "She could be concealing something there. I promised Dad to protect you. If you won't turn yourself in, the least you can do is search her."

"I'm not. Hiding anything, that is." Cher couldn't quite keep the humor from her tone because she understood his emotion. The whole agency had been frustrated by the woman. Her complaining was epic, and the ability to somehow shirk her duties the stuff of legend.

"See. She's not hiding anything."

Though Cher couldn't see Terri's face from where she stood, she imagined the petulant downturn to the other woman's lips she'd witnessed many times.

Ethan blew an audible breath speaking of long-held frustration. "Do you trust her?"

"Yes. I do. If she says she's not, she's not."

Cher added a little stamp of Terri's foot in her imagination.

He hauled Cher to a side chair, one with planks of oak for arms and cushions over the wood frame. "Sit."

She perched on the chair's edge, since the angle would be awkward with her hands behind her back. So, no crotch or breast search. Too bad she hadn't stuck the knife under her breasts along the band of her bra. She tried to imagine stuffing the sat phone up her hoo-ha like a couple of stories she'd heard from the agents, but her legs squeezed together in protest and she fought a squirm. No way.

The gargoyle stared at her from the couch. With his fingers laced together, he examined her like a dwarf examined a vein of pure fae gold.

Far be it from her to bother his rude review.

"So, Agent Cher Velasco," he said, his tone equitable, as if they were discussing the taxonomy of the fae, "you knew who I was from the start, didn't you?"

# CHAPTER 6

Across the cabin's seating area, Cher leveled her gaze against Ethan's. "I knew exactly who you were."

He blinked, not expecting her honesty. "Then you came here to arrest us."

She canted her head and her mouth flattened. "I said I wasn't here to arrest you. I can't. I'm an analyst, not an agent."

He flipped a glance over his shoulder to where his sister stood, behind the kitchen's peninsula, half-turned toward the door as if she wanted to flee into the coming blizzard clad in only her jeans and sweater. "Can she arrest you?"

Terri bit her lip, then said, "I don't know."

He turned his focus back to Cher in time to see her eye roll. Obviously, the tiny woman didn't think much of his sister. "What?"

"If I could've arrested you, you would've been in custody two nights ago. I would've come with a team to get Terri and not on an apparently unreliable snowmobile in the middle of a winter storm."

Her comment made sense.

"Besides," she continued with a head tilt and a you-must-be-really-dense expression, "I knew Terri could recognize me. I didn't even want to come inside. Just drop the box Grandmother sent me with and go back to her nice warm house, where I can make sure she doesn't fall or slip into a diabetic coma or have a heart attack and die while her nurse is on a week-long break." Her lids narrowed. "And where I'm not held captive at gunpoint."

The comment rankled, mainly because he didn't know Ms. Two-Birds was so fragile, though he could've guessed with her age-hunched stature and walker. The middle-aged woman who was at the ranch house when he came for the key must've been the nurse. Dammit, Cher was trying to protect her own family. Guilt began to eat at him, and he shifted on the cushions. "The gun's not on you now."

"But it's in the back of your waistband." Her brittle, knowing smile caught him off guard.

Wait a minute. She'd shifted the focus from her to him. He took his scattered thoughts and pushed the guilt to the side for now. "What's your talent? Or do you have more than one?"

"Just one. I see patterns and clues and fit them together." Her rueful smile could've spoken of a wish to have one more powerful.

The ability must've been how she put together who he was, though if she had a file on Terri, she probably didn't have to work all that hard. He needed a plan. "When should we expect agents to arrive?"

Cher's lashes swept down, then she pulled her direct, clear gaze back up. "I don't lie, so I'm not going to answer that question."

He wasn't sure if he should admire her honesty or be angry she wouldn't give him the truth. "You have called them, correct?"

"I'm not going to answer that question." Her chin lifted, and she glared down her pert nose at him, as if daring him to make her blurt all the details.

Since he'd never laid a hand on a woman, or anyone who hadn't aggressed on him first for that matter, Ethan had little choice but to accept her answers. He'd assume she had. He rose and shoved his index finger at her to emphasize his words. "Stay there."

She raised an eyebrow with her smirk. "Where am I going to go? Out into the snowstorm in only a sweater and jeans with my arms tied behind my back?"

The uncomfortable knowledge settled into his bones that he had, indeed, just made his sister's situation worse. He turned away, knowing what he had to do, but he wanted to tell Terri privately first.

"In your bedroom, please."

His sister's mouth hung slack for a moment, then snapped shut. "What? Why?"

"We need to talk." He didn't have time for her wide-eyed, little-girl expression.

Once in the bedroom, he shut the door, instinctively knowing—trusting—Cher would stay put.

Terri sat on the bed with her head bowed. Her voice was small and miserable. "What are you going to do with her?"

"What do you think I'm going to do?"

Her blue eyes flashed up to his, then went back to her hands, which were twisting in her lap. "Kill her?" she asked in a bare whisper.

Irritation snaked through him. He'd hoped she knew him better than as a murderer. "No. No killing."

With an audible breath, she lifted her head. Her eyes brimmed with tears.

"I'm going to let her go." Once he said the words he felt as if he'd made the right decision for the first time since this whole mess started. Would she accept his declaration?

Terri nodded slowly.

"It's better if you give yourself up anyway. I'll take my lumps for hiding you and kidnapping Cher. That was my stupid choice and shouldn't fall on you." Damn his father, but he still had to protect his sister and this was the only way he could now.

With tears streaming down her face, Terri rose and threw her arms around him and hugged him hard. "I'm so sorry," she chanted over and over through her sobs.

He returned her embrace. "We're going to be okay." Relief replaced the irritation, but then dread forced its way to the fore. How many years would he spend in jail for trying to keep his word to his father?

Finally, his sister's crying subsided, she disengaged, and with hunched shoulders, she turned from him to face the snow-obscured window. "Thank you. You didn't have to help me. I was so stupid."

He laid a hand on her shoulder and squeezed gently. Despite the impending jail time, the freedom on his shoulders felt like wings. "You were trying to help me in your own way. I wish you hadn't but it's done, and we'll figure out the best way to handle it. Running never was the right answer."

She nodded twice and her head hung with the second dip.

With a quiet snick, he shut the door and returned to the living area.

Cher had remained where he'd left her, as he knew she would, but she did so with a defiant tilt to her head.

Could he blame her? "Stand up, please."

"Why?" Fear crept into her eyes.

Suddenly very tired of all the hiding and deception, he said, "I'm going to free you."

She rose, taking her time. Calculation replaced the fear when she gained her feet. "Free me?"

"Yes. Turn around."

A triumphant smile growing on her face, she brought her hands from around her back and presented them to him. A long loop hung from one wrist. "No need."

*What the...* He stepped back and stood for a moment, his mouth dry, focus locked on the rope with its knot. Finally, he was able to manage words. "How…"

"If you're going to tie someone up, make sure there's nothing between the wrist and the binding. It can give enough room to slide the rope off." She waggled her forearms where her dense wool sweater's cuffs had been pushed up. The skin on her wrists and hands exhibited a bit of red where she'd probably rubbed them while removing the first loop.

Admiration warred with guilt for having ordered Terri to tie her up in the first place. "Smart."

She nodded, as if her intelligence was a given. "It just tells me y'all aren't into the whole kidnapping thing."

"A rookie mistake?"

"Something like that." She flashed him a brilliant smile, the kind he'd pay all the money in the world to see over and over again.

He joined her rich, husky chuckle. The shared moment intimate, his gaze tangled with hers, and his breath hitched. Desire spiraled thick and hot through his body.

Terri's door opened behind him, slamming him back to reality. He would be arrested and imprisoned by the very agency which employed Cher.

He swung away and pushed a hand through his hair as if the action would wipe away the attraction he felt toward this petite, curvy female. Correction—this gorgeous, smart-alecky, brilliant, petite, curvy female.

Terri joined him at the end of the kitchen peninsula where he faced Cher. "I'm going to see if I can get your snowmobile running. I didn't understand how bad off your grandmother was. If she died because you weren't there, I'd never forgive myself."

Cher's mouth formed an 'O', her fingers laced together hard, and she brought them to her mouth then down to her chest. "Thank you so much. She's a regular human and is having trouble with her diabetes medication right now. I'm pretty worried about her. I can take a jaunt for a couple of hours and run to the grocery store, but that's all I dare. Can I help?"

He glanced outside, where the snow had yet to begin falling, and headed toward the door. "I don't think so. I'm pretty good with engines. If it were one of the newer electric starts, I doubt I would get it going."

"Do you mind if I call my grandma?"

His hand on the door's knob, he stopped. The cabin had no landline, and cell phones didn't work out here. "Call?"

"With the sat phone. She keeps two—one for her, one for the nurse. I have the nurse's."

Fury slammed into him. But he'd searched her. She lied to him that she'd had nothing on her.

"I didn't lie to you," she said with caution in her tone. "It's in my snowsuit. Along with my fae knife, by the way."

He scrolled through the earlier events. She'd taken off the suit before he searched her, and stupidly, he didn't notice. "Another rookie mistake?"

She tilted her head with a crooked sorry-'bout-that smile.

"I've learned so much today," he said with a sheepish head shake.

"What are y'all talking about?"

When he turned his focus to his sister, Terri's gaze bounced between Cher and him.

"Long story." He shut the door and started whistling a tune his mother used to sing when she was cooking.

For the first time since Terri's madcap decision to betray a coworker and violate the law, he felt like he could control his fate.

# CHAPTER 7

C her hung up the phone and stared out the back window where Ethan crouched next to her snowmobile, his shirt rolled up to his elbows.

*Umm…strong forearms.*

She had no mechanical inclination, so other than him checking the spark plugs, she didn't know the fuel line from the carburetor, if the thing even had one. Useless. She'd be useless, but she wanted to go outside and help, if just to be next to him.

To smell his fresh scent.

To revel in the heat of his body.

Whoa.

She shoved away the desire building between her thighs. He was a suspect. Subject to charges for his actions. She could have nothing to do with him without losing her job. No job meant no ability to pay for a full-time nurse for her grandmother.

Family. She needed to focus on her grandmother. That's why she came home.

Abuelita had said she was fine and would be sure to

monitor her blood sugar. Cher tried to convince herself she wouldn't be so unlucky that tragedy would strike when she was stuck on the other side of the ranch. The device attached to her grandma's arm should alert them when her blood sugar fluctuated. Cher would get a ping on the sat phone as would her abuela. Hopefully the medical condition wouldn't be a major problem while Cher was away.

"How's your grandmother? She seems so nice." Terri shut the oven's door, into which she'd just slid the King Ranch casserole. She'd been unusually subdued over the last couple of minutes. Cher hadn't heard what was said between brother and sister behind the closed door, but once Terri emerged, Cher almost didn't recognize her. The sulky little girl had been replaced by some somber woman. Her bloodshot eyes and the blotches on her cheeks spoke of tears. Possibly, Terri finally understood she had a fate she must face.

A fate Cher didn't envy. The woman would go to jail, and probably wouldn't be released on bond since she'd fled once. A niggle of guilt wormed into Cher's conscious. While the NAC prison had state-of-the-art paranormal protection, the possibility existed someone might ensure the bounty became known within the jail. After all, Terri had pissed off half the organized crime families in the paranormal world with no hope of paying them back.

Cher banished the guilt. Well, mostly. The Porters had to have known what they faced by fleeing. But Terri had just asked about Cher's grandma. "I think she's fine. For now."

A wistful smile, both nostalgic and sad, crossed her face. "She was so nice when Ethan helped with the cow that escaped, and then when her nurse's car had a flat. Sent over some really great casseroles."

He'd helped grandma and her nurse? Why would his assistance surprise her? He was trying to help her now.

Terri stood square, facing Cher, with her hands folded in front of her. "I feel horrible that we kept you from her when she needs you."

"It's the snowmobile that trapped me here initially. Not you." Now why did she get all nice to the woman? Though Cher had spoken the truth, Terri had been such a pain in everyone's backside, most wouldn't be inclined to assuage the woman's guilt. Why did Cher?

Terri offered a shy half-smile in acceptance of Cher's words, then the expression died. "I-I want you to know that I'm done running." Terri's words rushed out, as if she didn't say them, she wouldn't follow her intentions. "I'm going right back to Enchanted Rock to turn myself in."

Wow. Though Cher couldn't be sure since she didn't read minds, everything in Terri's body language said she told the truth. Cher responded in kind. "All you have to do is wait here. They'll be in right behind Ernest's plow."

Something akin to terror flared in Terri's eyes, replaced quickly with drooped-shouldered resignation. "Easier, I guess."

"Nothing about accepting what you did wrong is easy. But, I think the prosecutors and the judge will see what you've done here, because I'm going to tell them you saw the error of running. That you apologized, Ethan set me free, and even helped my grandmother. You aren't evil. You made a bad choice."

If someone had told her she'd ever stand up for Terri Porter, Cher would've called them a liar. Especially since she really liked Talia Johnson, the woman whose information Terri sold.

A fat tear rolled down Terri's cheek, and her chin wobbled. "I don't know if I deserve that."

"I speak the truth, Terri. Everyone deserves the truth. It's why I do what I do."

"Truth is I was a pain in everyone's ass."

"Yeah." Cher couldn't argue, but did smother the rising snicker.

Terri dropped her gaze to where her hands were clasped together on the counter. "I'm sorry for that. I was such a..."

Cher waited for her to continue, maybe divulge why she acted like an overgrown, spoiled, sulky thirteen-year-old, but the other woman's lips sealed shut, and she turned her head to the kitchen window.

From outside, an engine turned over but didn't catch. Wait. The sound had none of the awful engine grinding from earlier. *My snowmobile!*

Cher raced to the back door.

Through the inset window, Ethen fiddled with a wire on the engine, then pulled the cord again.

The engine roared to life.

She'd pushed the worry to the side while dealing with the impossible situation, and now relief washed over her, humming in time with the engine's cycling. She opened the door to race outside, but closed it again. Wet socks in this weather was an invitation to frostbite, no matter how protective her boots. Instead, she grinned like a maniac through the window and shot him a thumb's up.

His boyish smile smacked her right in the heart. He sprinted up the stairs, and she made way for his entry.

Once he'd shut the door, he turned and clapped his hands on her upper arms. "I got it!"

"I noticed." The stupid-happy smile just wouldn't leave her face. The bright light in his blue-gray eyes mesmerized her. Her heart caught on the moment then began to beat again, this time slamming against her ribcage.

"Um..."

Terri's hesitant noise brought Cher crashing back to reality.

*What are you doing?* an internal voice demanded. *He's a suspect. Get home to your grandma.*

Mentally cursing herself, Cher turned and grabbed the wad of water-resistant, insulating fabric Terri offered her. At the dining table, she stepped into the overalls, yanking up the chest placket. A large male hand delivered one then the other strap, which she fastened to the buttons high on her chest. In short order, she'd tied her boot laces and snatched at her coat, which Ethan also handed her. She shoved her arms into the holes and started the zipper.

He put his hands on her shoulders, and the weight unexpectedly settled her. She raised her gaze to where he studied her with concern in his eyes. "You okay?"

"Yeah." Her annoyance had nothing to do with him. Well, at least *his* actions. She chose to mistake the implications behind his question. "I'll make it easily before dark. Should only be about a forty-minute trip."

He opened his mouth as if to say something, then shut it again. "Be careful."

She didn't—couldn't—meet his eyes, and chose a nod instead. A quick loop with her arms and her goggles were on. She shoved her hair into her hood and finally affixed the neck gaiter.

Once outside the cabin, she swung a leg over the seat, settling her ass into the decades-old groove. A quick glance to the west showed the bank of clouds hadn't moved much, so the storm should hold until she got home. Even a big eagle drifted by in the snowless sky.

She turned her head toward the cabin where Ethan and Terri came to the porch and stood side by side. The other woman raised an awkward hand, which she quickly lowered.

Ethan might as well have been made of stone for all the emotion he showed.

Cher echoed Terri's salute and turned the accelerator. The machine began to crawl, then picked up a little more speed, and she focused on the trail. No room for error. If she missed the path, she might end up stuck in a drift or a snow-filled depression.

At the rise, she stopped and took one last glance at the cabin. Terri had gone inside, but Ethan remained on the porch, barely distinguishable at this distance.

She committed the picture to memory—how the cabin's dark brown logs rose from the white blanket draped against them, how the smoke from the potbelly stove curled and lazed against the gray sky, how the big eagle circled above the cabin…

The eagle.

She glanced around. Everything—rabbits, marmots, deer, birds—had hunkered down for the storm. What was an eagle doing aloft spending precious energy resources?

Her heart hit her stomach and continued to plummet.

She drove on, entering the tree line. Once she made the next clearing, she stopped, tunneled into the placket of her coat, continuing to the overalls' front pocket and her satellite phone. On the first inhale without the gaiter over her mouth, the air knifed into her lungs. Fortunately, the wind had picked up and would whip away her words. She tugged off a glove, selected a number she'd recently dialed, and hastily returned her hand to its cocoon.

"Intel. Russell."

Good. She trusted Russell for the most part. She had to suck on her mouth to find enough moisture to swallow the lump in her throat. "It's Velasco. I called in the location of Terri and Ethan Porter, but was told no one could get up here for two days. Did someone get sent out for aerial surveillance?"

If not NACS, there'd be trouble.

"Lemme check."

Cher held her breath, knowing the answer full-well in her heart.

"Nope. No one yet. Looks like they've scheduled a team to be there tomorrow."

"Thanks." Crap. Crap. Crap. The bad guys had found the Porters. She hung up, then called the only person she would trust with this information—her best friend.

Ro Nlongo answered on the second ring, her tone cheerful. "What's up?"

"I have a problem." In the blustery wind, her lips had become as frozen as her words.

Ro must've detected the no-bullshit gravity in Cher's voice, because the agent's tone turned to all business. "What's the situation?"

"Remember I told you I found Terri and Ethan Porter?"

"Yeah. You called it in. I'm on the team. We're jumping in tomorrow when the storm abates."

"There are eyes in the sky above their cabin."

"What?" The word extended, indicating Ro's confusion.

"There's an eagle shifter circling above the cabin."

"We don't have an eagle—fuck."

"Yep." No eagle shifters in NACS. Cher mentally added a couple of curses on top of Ro's.

"Ideas on who it might be?"

"Nope." Cher licked her dry lips. "Take your pick from the myriad of crime bosses pissed at Terri. It gets worse." She waited for her friend to catch up to the logical conclusion.

"Worse?" Ro paused, then inhaled a sharp . Her voice cut

like glass. "Some asshole in NACS has been bought for information."

"As soon as I call it in, up they pop? Too convenient." How the leaker got around the blood vow like Terri did, Cher had no idea. But, where there was a will, there was a way, especially in the paranormal world. Every couple of months it seemed all the employees were having to re-up on that vow, and the NACS mages had to defend against a new workaround.

The swearing on the other end of the line would make a succubus blush. "I'm going to start at the top with this. Getting there due to the storm will be a problem, but we'll figure out a way. What's your plan?"

Since NACS fucked this up, it was up to NACS—Cher—to make it right. Plus, if the hitmen knew about the Porters, Cher and her grandmother could be at risk. "I'm going to continue on, like I'm going home and double back when it gets close to dark. And I'll pray they don't have an owl shifter to take over for the eagle." The storm would be upon her then, but she'd have to risk they'd continue the aerial surveillance despite the blizzard conditions. The idea made her shiver, and not from the cold.

"Unless he has a better arsenal, all we'll have is a gun and a fae knife." Cher continued, clamping down on the urge her teeth had to chatter. "There are no defenses here, so I'm taking them to the ranch house. You've been there. You can vortex the team at least to the Taos substation." How they'd get to Chama, let alone the ranch mystified Cher.

The idea froze her to her core, and she had to take several deep breaths to dispel the dizziness. Her visit today could bring mob retaliation to her grandmother. She nearly turned and hightailed it home. But, she couldn't let these two people get slaughtered. He'd helped her grandmother. Plus, Cher made the call to NACS. She would make it right if she could.

"A gun? Yours?"

"I'll tell you later." Best to gloss over that for now. "I'll let you know when we're at the ranch house. You might want to grab a couple of extra agents. This might get messy." She banished the fear creeping like slime down her spine. No time now to be scared.

Silence reigned for so long, Cher pulled the phone away to see if the signal had dropped. When she put it back to her ear, she said, "Ro?"

"Yeah." Her friend's voice was as taut as overstretched wire. "You don't have to do this you know. You're not an agent. Those two picked their own potion. I don't want you having to swallow the poison too."

"I know." She didn't have Ro's lion-shifter strength. Nor could she lob a mage's spells, or ride a ley line like a fae. She didn't have a demon's speed either. Just a pathetic Human Paranormal with self-defense training and a hellova dead-eye with a gun. But if she had a gargoyle on her side, they might have a chance.

"It's been a while since I've been to the ranch, but I'll have to chance my memory for the vortex. Give me a couple of hours to get everyone together. Can you hold on that long?"

"I'll have to. I just can't leave them to be murdered. My call allowed the bad guys to find the Porters. They have no idea what's inbound."

"You're a good egg, Cher Velasco."

"Yes, ma'am." Cher modified her tone to suggest she might've added a snappy salute with her words.

She signed off and tucked the phone away, Ro's last words ringing in her ears.

'Don't get yourself scrambled.'

# CHAPTER 8

E than closed the door to the potbellied stove and glanced at the pile of wood in the holder. He'd have to go out and get more soon. Even though the cold didn't bother him, he didn't relish digging around in the snow for wood with the wind driving flakes at thirty miles an hour.

So much for going flying tonight. He'd get blown around in the gale and smack himself unconscious against a tree or boulder.

They'd lost power twenty minutes ago, right as dusk began to descend and the snow fell like a deluge. The lights flickered, but other than the dull cycling of the compressor, he wouldn't have had any indication the diesel generator had kicked on. He'd turned off the electric baseboards and told Terri to put on an extra clothing layers. If they had to rely on the generator, they had no reason to draw more power with heaters than necessary. The age of the cabin said it had been constructed before electricity made it this far into rural America. If they could do with stove heating way back when, Terri could too. Out of the wind, the temperature sure as hell didn't bother him.

She huddled on the couch under a quilt, unusually quiet after Cher left. Less pouty about the heat than he expected too.

"You okay?"

She nodded. Her chin brushed her knees where it had been resting. "Just thinking."

Thinking? "About what?"

"How much I messed up." She straightened and brought her clear and direct gaze to his. Honesty? "How much I messed up everything for you."

He shifted on the cushion. "Yeah, well, you got the Sundas paid off. No use dwelling what it cost. That water under the bridge is long gone by now."

She shook her head. "No. I was selfish. I am selfish. I never look before I jump off that cliff, probably because I always expect someone to be there to catch me. But now I've gotten you in trouble. I'm going to make it up to you. Somehow, I will. I promise."

"Okay, Terri-Berry." Though he'd heard many of her promises in the past, this didn't seem like one she'd break. Luckily, she wasn't a gargoyle.

Her wobbly, lopsided smile held nostalgia. "You haven't called me that in years."

He swallowed his reply—he hadn't used the name because the woman she'd become wasn't the girl he grew up with. "The casserole smells delicious."

She threw off the blanket, crossed to the kitchen, and peered into the oven. "I think it's done." She twisted the temperature dial and grabbed a set of hot pads.

He hadn't been lying. Ethan's taste buds fired up when she'd opened the appliance and the full, spicy aroma hit his senses. "I'll grab the—"

A furious knocking sounded at the door.

*Someone found us.* He immediately reached to his back waist-band, but he'd already put the gun in his bag up in the loft.

"Ethan! Terri!"

Cher? His mouth dried. Why had she returned? Could she be setting them up? The idea didn't seem right. He hadn't heard the snowmobile. Maybe it quit on her?

"Let me in. It's important."

The desperation in her tone spurred him from where his feet had cemented to the floor.

He sprinted to the door and yanked it open, leaving room for her to rush by along with blowing flakes and frigid wind. As soon as he could, he slammed the door shut.

Despite his pleasure in seeing her again, why was she here?

She jerked off her gloves while she raced to the stove then held her bared hands toward the warmth. "D-Damn, is it c-cold out there."

She hadn't bothered to pull up her goggles, and she still wore her hood. Snow clung to her entire body, crusting to her visor, forming clumps and freezing to the suit where it would've collected when she sat on the snowmobile.

"Why are you here? Did the snowmobile quit on you?" Terri's tentatively voiced concern surprised him. Perhaps she really did have a change of heart.

Cher massaged her hands and turned around to face them, pulling her jacket's gaiter from her mouth. "I—" Her words were cut off by her teeth's chattering.

"Why don't we get you out of those layers, so you can get warm by the stove." He started toward her.

She shook her head vehemently. "No t-t-time." She took a deep breath. "I saw a shifter in the sky as I left earlier. Get only what you need. We have to go."

A shifter. Rocks seemed to bounce around in his stomach. "Not NAC Security?"

"No." The word's finality hit like two-tons of solid gargoyle fist.

Of course not. She would've thought of that already and probably checked in with her office. Someone—not just someone, an assassin—had found them. But one shifter wouldn't be enough against a gargoyle. Surveillance meant a larger group would storm the cabin.

"Go?" Terri said slowly. "Where are we going to go in this weather?"

"To the ranch house." Cher seemed to be warming up. Her movements were less jerky and her speech more fluid and less like her tongue had frozen solid. She turned her focus to him. "Bring your gun and whatever other weapons you have. Wear your warmest gear, but bring nothing else. We're traveling light."

Terri stood stock still, as if her predicament's dire nature had yet to register. "I-I don't have anything like...like that." She circled her finger at Cher in her offensively-orange, snow-blotched winter gear.

"Doesn't matter," Ethan said. "Throw on three of your thickest sweaters. I have a rain jacket that you can wear over top to keep the wind and the wet from you. Long johns. I think you have those. Get them on too."

He'd fly unburdened to fight. Hopefully, he wouldn't bash himself unconscious in the high winds.

Incredulity creeped across his sister's features. "You're serious? How are we going to get there?"

"Snowmobile." Cher said. "You'll ride behind me. I'll take the worst of it. If you have a scarf, wrap it around your head and face under a hat until only your eyes are showing. Sunglasses, too, if you have them."

Terri froze. "You *are* serious."

Cher had patience, while he had none remaining. All of them must get out now. He had to protect his sister.

*Dammit, get her moving.* "As dead serious as in you'll be dead if we don't get out of here soon. Once the storm dies down, they could send in avian shifters, polar bears, wolves, demons, gargoyles, and whoever else can make it here through the snow." He crossed to his sister and gave her shoulders a little push in the direction of the bedroom. "Get moving, Terri. You have ten minutes."

The slight contact seemed to allow the words to penetrate and horror blossomed across her face. She scurried to her room, tossing over her shoulder, "I'll be ready."

He pivoted and sprinted up to the loft, where he grabbed a bag and threw in his other pair of hiking boots, his wallet, and a change of clothes, since he wouldn't wear anything but pants when he flew. Last in was the extra gun he had, plus the spelled, fae silver bullets which had cost him a damn fine penny. The rounds may not kill those from Clans Shifter, Sanguis, or Fae, but they'd sure make them wish they'd died.

He grabbed his rain jacket last, then pounded down the stairs.

Cher had brushed off the snow onto the ancient braided rug and now stood next to the stove with her coat hanging open.

For a moment, he stared at her, unsure what to say when she'd sacrificed so much to come back. "Why did you do this? You could've left us to our fate just as easily and been home safe."

She stared at her toes, then her golden gaze lifted to his. "I couldn't leave you two to die or whatever they would've done to you. We'll have a better chance at the ranch house."

The ranch. Where her grandma lived. Then her true sacrifice hit him, and he stared at her while words failed him.

Finally, he said, "You can't just bring these people to your grandmother's house."

"By the surveillance just seeing me put her in danger. She has a safe room my dad had installed. He…angered someone back in the day. They could burn the house down, drop a nuclear bomb on it, and we'd all be safe." A flash of disquiet flew across her face. "Unless, of course, they had a way to access it, which I doubt."

Damn. He hadn't even known Ms. Two-Birds was connected to the paranormal world and he hadn't considered his and Terri's mere connection to her might put her in danger. "I didn't detect your grandmother's clan."

"No clan. Her daughter married an HP." A quirked smile flitted to her lips. "I got watered-down fae genes. Dad's dad was a gremlin. Can't you tell by my petite stature?"

Gremlin? He took in her body, then met her gaze letting a bit of the hunger he'd experienced earlier shine his eyes, just as he'd seen in hers when they first encountered each other. He murmured, "Looks gorgeous to me. And fae would explain your expressive eyes. Sometimes they're hazel, sometimes green, sometimes gold, like they are now."

She dropped her gaze and started to zip up her coat. "We should be going."

Had he mistaken her flashes of interest? Probably. What would she be doing with a wanted gargoyle anyway? She was too smart for that.

Terri, or a puffy version of Terri, who was swathed in sweaters and scarves and sunglasses, rushed out of her room carrying downy mittens and a wool coat. "Is this enough?"

Cher gave her the once over. "It's got to be."

"Put your purse in here." He handed Terri the bag and followed up with the jacket.

She dutifully put her purse in the bag and tried to give the duffle back to him.

He held up his hands. "You'll have to wear it crossbody behind you." With the confused wrinkle to her brow, he added, "I'm going to have to fly and will need as much mobility as possible. The guns are in there. Safety's on. They're loaded with spelled, fae silver bullets."

As if she held a hissing cobra, she pushed out her hands at arms-length. "I don't know how to shoot a gun."

"I do." Cher made grabby hands toward Terri, who turned over the duffle. A quick rummage and she pulled out one of the large handguns, which seemed to swamp her petite stature. She smiled, the grim crescent promising hellfire for anyone she targeted. "A forty-five with spelled bullets? My favorite."

Of course she'd know how to handle a gun.

She stuffed the pistol in the pocket of her coat, then handed the bag back to his sister. "Put the other gun in your pocket."

Terri accepted the duffle reluctantly. "But I don't know to use it."

Cher hefted a breath then stepped to Terri, snatched the bag back, and pulled the other forty-five from within. After a couple of quick maneuvers, she'd removed both the magazine and ejected the round from the chamber. "Hold it in your hand."

Terri's head swiveled back and forth vehemently.

His sister hated guns. That's why he asked her to tie Cher up earlier. "I don't know if she can do this."

Cher's eyes flashed green from behind narrowed lids. "This could be the difference between living and dying. Even if she doesn't hit a damn thing, it could keep them at bay. Stop treating her like a child."

Cher's focus turned back to Terri, who stared at the gun in

Cher's hand as if it would gobble her whole. "I don't have time to sugarcoat this. You made a huge mistake. Other people's lives are on the line now. Time for you to put on your big-girl panties. Take the damn gun."

While Cher's words were harsh, her tone had gentled.

Miraculously, Terri took the weapon in her hand.

"Squeeze the grip harder. This thing will have a kick like a bull moose and jump out of your hand if you're not holding it tight. Two hands are best. Now, here's the safety." Cher's tone had become brisk and efficient as she pointed out the feature. "It's on 'safe' right now and won't fire. Flip this lever down with your thumb and it will. Three things I need you to remember. One, do not take it off 'safe' until you are ready to shoot at something. Repeat it to me please."

Though she'd paled, Terri repeated the first of Cher's rules. That she seemed to assent to Cher's demands made him wonder if Cher had been right. Had he been treating Terri too much like a child?

"Two. Keep your finger off the trigger until you are ready to shoot at something. Please repeat that." Once Terri complied, Cher continued, "Three, never point a gun at something you don't want to shoot."

After Terri dutifully repeated the third rule, Cher took the weapon back, reinserted the magazine, fed a round into the chamber, then replaced the fed round with the extra to make a full magazine once more. Her efficiency and ease with the pistol spoke of long familiarity.

His admiration for her grew. "How long have you been shooting?"

"About as long as I've been alive. I often go to the range with my best friend." She handed the automatic pistol back to his sister, holding the weapon by the barrel. "When accepting a gun, make sure you know what state it's in. You saw me load it, so you know it's ready to fire. Make sure the safety's on."

Terri accepted the pistol and checked the safety. While trepidation still lurked in her eyes, her grip seemed more sure, as if she believed she might be able to squeeze the trigger if she had to.

Who was this person in his sister's form?

And who was this miracle worker named Cher?

She turned to him, her gaze grave with the risk she bore. "You ready? It's windy out there, so watch your wings."

A lump had grown in his throat, one built of guilt for involving her in the first place, guilt for not being able to keep his sister safe, and fear for this woman he knew he would woo if things were different. All he could do was jerk a nod.

And pray they made it to the ranch house alive.

# CHAPTER 9

L est a sharp-eyed predator picked out the beam, Cher didn't dare use the light as she negotiated the icy, treacherous path. The machine's noise was bad enough, though hopefully the near gale-force winds would muffle the engine. The snow amplified the difference between light and dark enough that she could traverse the trail she'd used her whole life without extra illumination. But at a cost. While she moved faster than she would've had she walked the distance, the journey seemed to move at a snail's pace.

She'd been driving for what seemed like an eternity, but in reality, for probably only forty-five minutes, already twice as long as it would normally take on a snowmobile. Anxiety clung to her throat, closing around the passage with a death grip, much like Terri's arms clutched her middle. Sweat already plastered Cher's thermal base layer to her body and her mittens to her hands. Her fingers had begun to tingle with cold. She eased open the throttle a fraction more—she had to get to the house before she lost a finger to frostbite. Plus, the appendages still had to work if she needed to fire her gun.

She wanted to see Ethan, but with the trees this close

around her and the pockets of deep snow and boulders on either side of the trail, she risked death if she diverted her attention. He wouldn't be able to fly this low with the branches closing overhead anyway. And when had just seeing him made her feel more centered? Hell, he could've flown off, leaving her and Terri to their fates.

No, he wouldn't. He said he'd promised to protect his sister. If he must, he'd be circling to keep up with the snowmobile's slow pace.

A hard bump had the machine fishtailing. She jerked the handles, struggling to get them back on course. Terri screamed in Cher's ear. For heart-squeezing moments, Cher fought the snowmobile's sideways slide at a drop-off's edge.

*Focus!*

With the machine once again under control, she emerged from a fir tree grove and into a small meadow. Her heart slowed and even lifted a bit. *One more tree-covered rise, and the long run down the valley to the ranch house and abuelita.* She could do this.

"Hey!" Ethan's voice came at her shoulder.

Though his yell brought her comfort, she wouldn't risk a glance from her path. "What?" she shouted back, pushing aside the sting from a lip which decided to crack.

"I heard wolves howling behind us. I think they found the cabin empty. We need to go faster if we can."

Her insides seemed to crystalize, and the snow mobile slowed a bit. *Fuck, fuck, and double fuck. No. We'll be okay—we're almost home.*

Nevertheless, she pulled on the throttle, past where she'd gone before. Sheer suicide at this rate. She cursed herself for doubling back to save the Porters, then cursed herself again for doubting her choice. If she had to die, she'd die doing the right thing.

*Drive.*

Tension piled on her shoulders like the deep drifts she plowed through. She crested the next rise. Never had the little valley where she grew up been such a welcome site. Due to farming and livestock grazing, most of the large rocks had been cleared, so she opened up the throttle and largely kept to where she knew the rutted path to exist.

Hard flakes knifed at her cheeks where the gaiter and goggles didn't quite meet. She wouldn't have thought it possible, but Terri hugged her harder, stealing the breath from Cher's body.

No time to complain. She steered the bucking machine toward the house over a half-mile away. The muted glow in the windows promised salvation and freedom from the crushing cold and the oncoming predatory jaws which would consume her.

"Hurry!" Ethan shouted. "They're getting closer."

Cher cursed. He'd have to stave off the pursuers at this speed. She may be able to pry her hands from the accelerator, but firing a weapon right now was out of the question. "Get ready to get that gun, Terri."

"O-Okay," the other woman said through chattering teeth. One arm left from her embrace, and the remaining hand clutched all the tighter around Cher's middle.

Finally, she reached the front porch. With a flick of her wrist she turned off the ride. Terri got off, moving slowly and probably half-frozen.

Cher didn't move much faster, but desperation grew. *Inside now.* She grabbed Terri's hand while Cher's other one was already bare and in her pocket grabbing the stowed gun. "Come on."

A canine snarl came from her right. Cher flicked the safety as she pulled the trigger at a ball of fur leaping toward them.

Terri's scream mingled with a high-pitched yelp which said

Cher had found the target, but she didn't stop moving her stiff limbs and yanked the other woman with her.

Her grandmother opened the door. Cher pushed Terri inside then slammed it shut so the other woman was safe. Cher would defend from outside until all were safe behind the wards she would trigger. Ethan remained at risk.

A blur came from her right, a blur with paws, not wings. She turned, fired two rounds. A squeal then gurgles. Good. Two down. The slightest wing flap gave warning and she trained her barrel on the sound.

Ethan.

Relief surged through her. She immediately lowered her weapon.

He landed and raced up the wooden stairs. His skin had transformed to a dark gray. Bare, muscled chest and arms. His ears were pointed, his blue eyes glowing. She'd never seen anything so powerful.

One wing dripped glittering, dark drops and a stain spread on his thigh.

Her breathing caught on the lump lodged in her throat. She choked out, "You're hurt."

"Get inside. There's a whole pack." His face twisted with a grimace.

She turned the door's handle and rushed inside with Ethan on her heels. She threw the lock and scrabbled at her neck gaiter, then tunneled under her sweater for her necklace. Her fingers were almost too cold to discern the shape, but she found the right pendant and held it to the door's heavy oak.

The amulet grew warm, like fire to her frigid fingers, and she released the platinum piece. She'd activated the ward. They should be secure enough to get to the real safe room. Her knees sagged with relief, and she leaned against the wall for support.

A thump, a sizzle, then an angry snarl sounded from the other side of the door.

Cher recoiled. She, Grandma, Ethan, and Terri crowded through the doorway on the right and into the living room with its big picture window. Large, long, dangerous shapes prowled outside in the blizzard. Cher picked out a polar bear and several wolves. Who knew what other type of shifter sought a way in?

*Doesn't matter. Check in with Ro and get to the safe room.*

She stuffed her second glove into her pocket and pulled out the satellite phone. At least the tech had stayed warm enough to function. A simple push and she reached Ro. "Shifters all the way up to polar bears," she said without even waiting for a greeting. "No real attack on the wards yet, but we're headed to the safe room. You know which stone is the doorbell. Give me five taps. We won't get reception there."

"The team's almost ready. We're waiting on our extra three fae. We're going to vortex into Taos. Hop a ley line to get closer. Secured a snowcat to get to you." Ro's voice held both concern and determination. "Stay safe."

"You too." A ley line? A fae could only bring one with them at a time, which would make bringing in a large team time-consuming. She shook her head to clear the negativity. Despite the travel complications, Cher had to believe the team would save them. The alternative would rob her of all will to continue.

She stowed the phone and turned to the three next to her. "Come on. To the safe room."

"Isn't this safe enough?" Terri asked through chattering teeth. She hugged her body, with her arms crossed around her middle, whether from cold or fright or a combination of both, Cher couldn't discern.

"This is a simple warding for an entire house." The sheer

size and the fact Cher, a non-magic wielder, set the protective spell with an amulet meant the ward was the most basic level. "It won't hold if they get even a half-assed witch or sorcerer or mage up here."

She eyed the drip-drip of shimmering blue blood from the tip of Ethan's wing, one he held closely to his body. His tight features suggested the bad guys probably had spelled, fae silver bullets too. "Plus the medical supplies we'll need are there."

Cher turned and guided her grandma to the den, next to the kitchen, where the older woman had already closed the curtains. "You've been busy, Abuelita."

She smiled, her teeth flashing white against her tanned skin, while her eyes sparkled behind her owlish glasses. "I fight in my own way, mija."

Grateful for her grandmother's spunkiness, Cher stepped up to the stacked-stone wall which held the fireplace. Her fingers had begun to swell and burn now as they warmed, but she pushed aside the pain to select another pendant, this time a moonstone with ancient fae characters engraved into the surface. She placed the gem against a small piece of granite, the one stone which could open the way into the safe room.

A bright light grew in a doorframe's shape to her right. Despite a fair amount of certainty the house's wards would hold until they got inside, tension stiffened her shoulders. Pops, hisses, and the occasional angry yowl sounded from outside as their pursuers tested the house's defenses.

Cher released a breath when her grandmother shuffled inside. Cher motioned to Terri and Ethan to follow, then she fell in behind them. Another press of the moonstone against the stacked stone pattern inside secured the door to the room which wasn't a real room within the house. Space compressed itself around the area, to make it more of a sub-dimension, essentially a tiny fae realm. At least, that's how her father had described the process. All of the remaining fae gold coins left by his father had gone into the construction. Who made the room and how were secrets he swore to keep. He took them to his grave.

Safe. They were finally safe. For a moment Cher felt nothing, not relief, not joy, then everything—the fear they'd be caught, the anxiety her grandmother would suffer a medical issue while she was gone, the terror Ethan would be killed—swamped her like the raging waters of a flash flood. Shaking, she sagged against the wall, sliding down the rough stone until she sat on her haunches with her face hidden in her hands. Bands tightened around her lungs, and she sucked for air as chills wracked her body.

Ethan hauled her up and enveloped her in his arms.

Blissful comfort came from his embrace. Her cheek rested against his bare chest and the warmth from his body felt like the midsummer sun. Within seconds, her shivering had ceased, and she began to breathe easier. She glanced up to his face, transformed by the shift to his gargoyle alter ego. His skin should be cold, hard, and unyielding, but under her fingers, he felt warm, silky smooth, and all male. His gaze held a wonder that caught her off guard.

Skin, not stone. His skin was *warm*.

Stories from her childhood, passed down from her father, collided in her brain. Her world shifted, and she clung to him, while a small, breathy internal voice chanted, *Oh shit. Oh shit. Oh shit.*

As if he recognized the same problem, he stiffened.

She rested her forehead against that skin and clutched his bare shoulders. On one level she gloried in the connection, while on a more logical level she grappled with the revelation.

She was Ethan's mate.

Only a mate would feel a gargoyle's true skin and not hard stone.

How could she be mated to a felon? Would he be a felon? How would he feel to be mated to someone he couldn't have? Could she find a legal job that paid as well as NACS? These and other panicked questions whirled around in her brain until they formed one single issue.

She was so screwed.

If only his skin would feel like granite so she could bang her head against it. But now she understood the crazy attraction. While HPs didn't feel a mating call or otherwise exhibit signs of who their life partner would be, some, like shifters and gargoyles, did.

"You know?" Ethan's low voice held an edge of concern.

She nodded and brushed her skin against his skin. Tears began to pool in her eyes. If only things were different. Her croaked, "Yep," managed to emerge despite the regret clutching her lungs.

"Know what?" Terri's question broke into the moment.

"Nothing," Ethan said faster than Cher could form a word or thought.

She tore herself away from him. Distance. She needed distance to think. He was a suspect. She'd taken an oath she would uphold justice and the reputation of the agency, which included not getting involved with suspects, let alone convicted felons. How could she even like him? Think he was sexy? Then she spied the drips of his blood on the tile merging into the good-sized glimmering puddle where he stood, his life's essence a sparkling blue against the brown floor.

Her heart stuttered in her chest, like a bird with a broken wing.

She used his injuries as a distraction to cover her whirling thoughts about her wild attraction to Ethan Porter, a possible suspect in aiding and abetting his sister's flight from prosecution. One of the four sets of shelves lining the wall of the thirty-by-thirty-foot room held medical supplies. The stacks stuck out and faced each other, creating separation from the sets of bunkbeds lined against the walls behind the provisions.

Without needing her encouragement, Ethan followed her. She pulled the heavy kit from the shelf, toted it to a table pushed against one of the walls, then pointed to a slatted chair in the front part of the room. "Sit."

A small smile seemed to tug at the corners of his mouth, but he dutifully sat, arranging his wings around the chair's back.

Across from him sat her grandmother, who looked a bit fatigued. Too much excitement in her day left Cher concerned. "Why don't you lie down, Grandma?"

Slowly, the older woman nodded. "I think I will."

Cher helped her grandmother to one of the lower bunkbeds placed against the long wall behind the shelves and settled a quilt over her. She laid her hand on the gnarled one atop the coverlet. The connection renewed Cher's strength. "Thank you for making me go."

Her insides warmed with her grandma's proud smile. "You always do the right thing."

*Ha.* Considering jumping the bones of a suspect was hardly the right thing to do, even if she was his mate. Dammit. She shoved that aside, patted her abuelita's hand, and resumed her position in front of the med kit. Hot. It was hot in here. And not just from Ethan. She unzipped her coat, then took it off and hung the puffy layer on the back of one of the chairs. "I take it you got hit with some spelled bullets and that's why you can't transform back?"

"Yep. My wings. And a through and through on my thigh."

If not for his confirmation and the brilliant blue drips which matched his eyes, Cher wouldn't have guessed he was injured. Only the faintest brackets around his mouth told how dearly he paid in pain.

"Ethan." Terri moved her hands from covering her eyes to her mouth. She pushed from her position where she leaned against the stacked stone wall and rushed over, kneeling next to him. "Why didn't you say anything?"

*I only mentioned it twice. Why didn't you notice?* Since the woman had been on a wild ride through a blizzard with a pack of paranormal organized crime hitmen at her heels, maybe Cher could cut her a break.

His shoulders lifted then fell back. "There's nothing I can do for the pain."

His gaze found Cher's. Something like promise glowed along with the blue in his eyes. "But she can help me now. She's the only one who can."

# CHAPTER 10

C her bit her lip, the very one he'd been dreaming about sucking on since he saw her. She turned and busied herself with the box of potions and standard first aid supplies.

Terri's gaze ping-ponged between Cher and him with her mouth lax. Finally, she said, "What do you mean, she's the only one who can?"

He shouldn't have said those words. Terri was clueless and needed to remain that way. The less people knew about the mating, the less likely the hitmen out there could use the knowledge against Cher and her grandmother. Plus, Cher probably thought he was trying to blackmail her. Maybe she thought he was asking her to let them go. Dammit. He'd explain to Cher he meant as his mate later. "The, uh, kit. She has the first aid kit."

Terri looked down. "I'm sorry I got you hurt." For a moment, he thought she would cry, but then her spine stiffened and she met his gaze once more. "I'm going to get you out of this. You don't deserve to be in trouble for my stupid mistakes."

If someone had told him he'd be proud of his sister today,

he'd have called the person a liar. He put his hand on her shoulder, careful to do so lightly. When he'd transformed to his gargoyle state, she, like most others, would experience the gargoyle's stone weight. "It will work itself out, Terri. No more harebrained ideas, please."

She rose from kneeling and shook her head. "Nope. I will only entertain well-thought-out ideas from now on."

For some reason, he believed her. If this was the price he paid for a change in Terri, one from a spoiled, inconsiderate princess who got bailed out of everything, he'd take it. The agony from the spelled bullets burned like dragon fire, but he could manage. He must. Not like he could wish away the pain. At least the bones in one of his wings had knit back from the break he'd suffered when a gust sent him into a tree.

Cher pulled out a small, instantly-recognizable, yellow-green bottle with a cork stopper.

*Ugh. Cure Now potion.*

"I think this is the best we can do. Not my favorite." She turned to him and gingerly took a hold of his damaged wing. Soft. Everything about her was soft, including her skin. Her fingers stroked down to the outer edge and pulled a bit. "Can you extend it? I think you were holding it awkwardly earlier."

He gritted his teeth against the sensation of her fingers skimming his wing's sensitive flesh. When a mate touched a gargoyle's wings, one thing came to mind—sex. All of their nerve endings led to one place for their mate.

He shifted in the hard seat as a flood of desire washed over him and tightened his jeans to a point almost more painful than the holes in what appeared to be delicate webbing.

"Ah…" He cleared his throat. "Yes, I can extend it."

Concerned hazel eyes flashed to his. "Sorry I'm hurting you."

"You're not." His voice came out as if spoken through gravel while he struggled to control his roiling senses.

Understanding's light dawned in her gaze. She licked her lower lip and averted her eyes. Once she removed her fingers from the webbing, and he wasn't sure whether to sigh with relief or regret.

Once he'd unfurled his wing, she bent down to examine the appendage. "Pretty bad tears in the lower portions. They're still bleeding and it will probably continue since the damage was due to the spelled bullets." She rose and she hovered her hand over the ugly-colored bottle, while she grimaced slightly, no doubt understanding the toll the Cure Now would take. "Do you want the potion?"

He considered the options. All-consuming pain for several minutes or awful pain for a couple of days plus remaining in gargoyle form? With the unknown enemy still out there and possibly able to break through, not to mention NAC Security's unknown arrival time, best to be at full strength. He held out his hand to Cher. "I'll take the Cure Now."

"I have a Revive Me potion for the backend." Her tone had become devoid of emotion, as if the last ten minutes, ten minutes where both she and he learned of the mating, mattered nothing to her. *Duh, of course it doesn't. She's an HP. And she probably still thinks you're trying to use the fact for leverage.*

He accepted the vilely-yellow bottle and uncorked the top. Before he knocked it back, he said to Terri, "Could you go check on Ms. Two-Birds?"

His sister's gaze shifted to the older woman, then back to him, then to Cher. Maybe she'd deduced he wanted to speak to Cher alone. Without a word, Terri crossed the room.

At least she didn't put up a fight. When she was sufficiently away, he turned to Cher. They couldn't part with her thinking he'd use her for his ends. "I didn't want you to think I meant anything or intended to use the fact that you're my mate as some sort of tool to let us go. You are under no obligation to me. The choices I've made and the repercussions are mine alone."

A bit of tension dropped from Cher's shoulders. "I didn't know what you meant when you said only I can help to Terri."

He put his hand over her small, delicate, capable one where it rested on the table. Would this be the last time he touched her? "My words came out wrong. I just hope that someday, you can see past what I did and at least try to get to know me."

Cher's lips opened as if she would say something, then confusion flitted across her face. She shook her head and gently slid her hand away. "I'm sorry, Ethan. I work for NACS. I'd be fired. I need the job for my grandmother. I can't be involved with a suspect or felon."

His heart stuttered at the finality in her voice. Just his dumb luck his mate would be the one person he couldn't have. He'd no more ask her to give up her career than he'd ask her to intercede for him and Terri. There had to be a way out of this mess so he could at least try to win her. He could already recognize his gargoyle had formed an attachment to her—her courage, her protectiveness for her grandmother, her sexy little body of which he wanted to explore every inch. He would figure this out, but before he went lights out for a bit, he had one more question.

"If I were not a suspect or felon, what then?" Ethan searched her expression.

He found a flare of heat before she quickly snuffed it out and turned toward the med kit, straightening some bottles, removing one more vial. She turned back to him, her expression wiped completely clean. "I deal in facts, Ethan. What is, not what may be. You *are* a suspect and may be a felon, so it's pointless to speculate."

If not for what he'd seen in her eyes before she turned away, he might've believed her. He tucked the golden flash of desire away in his memory banks. The moment would be his motivation to do whatever it took for him to taste her mouth, see humor curve her generous lips, and convince her she was his mate, and he hers.

Certain of his mission, he tipped up the bottle's end and downed it in one gulp. Nothing. Huh. He set the vial on the table. Maybe the sweet potion was too old to—

A nuclear bomb exploded from within, firing all of his nerve endings to sizzling, agonizing flame. He clamped his lips shut against the lightning which arced through him. A small part of him recognized he'd fallen to the floor, his back arching, his body struggling against the rapid healing potion's torture.

Blackness.

# CHAPTER 11

"Are you sure he's going to be okay?" Terri stared at her brother where he lay twitching on the safe room's floor. She clasped her hands tightly, leaving her knuckles white.

Cher gazed down at Ethan, apprehension gripping her guts. She should've had him lie down on one the beds, but he'd distracted her with his questions. And his hope. Stupid and too late now. Better to not get close while the potion worked. He'd flailed as he spasmed and slid from the chair to the floor. One blow from him could seriously wreck her or Terri's day. "He'll be fine."

He had to be. Though she'd told him there could never be anything between them, she felt the pull of the mating deep within. Something in her distant fae genes seemed to acknowledge him. Gargoyles weren't as despondent as shifters when they couldn't have their mates, but for him to know the perfect one was out there walking the earth and not be able to be with them was torture enough without getting full-on shifter hormones involved.

He moaned and rolled to lay on his back—on his wings, really—but enough of the surprisingly delicate webbing still showed to indicate his injuries had healed. Once the potion worked, the healing pain faded and he should be safe to approach, even if he remained unconscious.

Relieved the worst of his agony had ended, she knelt with the Revive Me potion in hand and glanced at Terri. "Help me lift him so I can get this down his throat."

Terri slipped her hands under one shoulder, tugged, and grunted. "Good grief, gargoyles are ridiculously heavy."

Cher changed to the other shoulder. She didn't think him especially weighty, but then she was his mate. "Just a second while I pour this down."

The potion fizzed against his lips. Dang it. She shifted to sit cross-legged behind him. "Okay, let's let him down. Grab a pillow from one of the beds, and we'll try to get his mouth open enough so he can swallow."

Cher slid the pillow between her legs and his head. He hadn't moved a muscle since the Cure Now, and she checked his breathing. His chest rose and fell as if he slept. He would continue to be unconscious for at least four more hours if left alone. While the Cure Now supposedly tasted sweet, akin to peanut brittle some said, Revive Me was vile, a cross between blood and bitter apple with a side of cigarette smoke. Cher had taken the latter potion in the past, and a shudder of distaste wriggled through her.

Gently, Cher smoothed back a curl which had fallen onto his forehead, wondering how he appeared so fierce when awake, but so gentle when asleep. If only she could summon a spell to remove all of this for him. But those spells didn't exist. The temptation to take him and run away nearly overwhelmed her.

Her gaze flew to Terri, who chewed on her lip. Maybe running was understandable if given the right circumstances.

*Enough,* her practical side said. *Give him the damn potion.*

With one trembling hand, she grasped his chin and pulled down enough to pour the Revive Me between his lips. A little trickled out of his mouth. He hadn't swallowed. "Stand back, Terri."

The other woman complied, and Cher did what she knew worked—held his mouth shut with one hand and pinched his nose closed with the other.

For a moment, he didn't respond. Then with a jerk, his arms flailed and his head turned from side to side probably trying to shake her loose. Cher held on with all her strength until his Adam's apple bobbed, and she released both hands.

He sputtered and coughed, then his eyes flew open and he stilled. His intense blue gaze caught hers, and a crooked smile snagged at her heart. "Hello."

His voice, rough and guttural, spoke of the last ten minutes of healing. The Cure Now potion used brutal magical tactics, stealing from the victim's own paranormal essence to over-whelm and reverse any spells or potions the victim had been subjected to, as well as to accomplish any physical healing required. Cher had never had to use it, thank God.

She stroked one of her hands down his cheek. "Hello your-self. How do you feel?"

"Like death licked an ashtray and spit me back out."

His exaggerated grimace made her want to giggle. "That good, eh?"

He wheezed a laugh, and pushed himself up so he sat facing her. "But better every second."

"Can you shift back yet?" The ability would indicate he'd truly been healed.

"Let's check." A burst of blue flared in his eyes, and then the paranormal glow faded, his skin changed, his fangs receded, and his wings disappeared. He glanced down at his bare arms, then at her. "Yep. Back to full-strength."

And just as sexy with all the bare skin skimming across his heavy muscles. Hard abs trailed to the waistband of his jeans. She swallowed, her mouth suddenly dry. "Ah…why don't we get you something to rinse out the Revive Me." *Before I lose my damn mind.*

"I'll get him some water."

How could Cher have forgotten Terri was right there? Denied the separation she needed to stay sane, she could only stare at him, at his perfect body and face and hair, like she'd ingested a love potion. He didn't help matters by gazing back, his heart in his eyes, telling her without words he wanted her like no other.

"Here ya go." Terri shoved the water bottle into his hand then straightened.

Her rough action startled Cher, and she shifted her focus to the other woman, who gazed down at her brother with narrowed, but not unkind, eyes. Had Terri guessed their secret? Best if she didn't know. She had a lousy track record with secrets.

*Stop mooning like a damn lovesick goat.* Cher bounced up to look for something to do, then her eyes lit on the bottom edge of the bunk, where the blanket-covered lump of her grand-mother's tiny feet were just visible around the shelves. Guilt flooded her. She should be more concerned with her abuelita than a fantasy love life which could go nowhere.

Cher crossed the short distance and gently lowered herself to the side of her abuela's bed. The older woman's face showed lines from the years of life, some grooves from laugh-ter, some from sorrow, all from a kind heart. "What is it, mija?"

Cher blinked. Her grandmother's eyes hadn't opened. Had she imagined the question?

The older woman turned her head, and her lids lifted

behind the thick lenses. A knowing smile curved her lips. "You needn't worry about me. You should go back to that fine young man."

Mortification lanced through Cher and she whispered, "Grandma!" Cher's gaze darted to Ethan, whose supernatural hearing should've picked up the conversation. No need for him to know he had a cheerleader in her abuela. Yet his focus on his sister hadn't deviated.

Her abuelita husked a dry chuckle, then whispered back, "From the moment I saw him, I knew he was the one for you."

If only... But her grandmother had to be her focus. Searching for an excuse—any excuse—to deny her grandmother's words, she blurt-murmured, "But he's married."

"He's not wearing a ring, she's not wearing a ring. I don't know their relationship, but it's not husband and wife." She patted Cher's hand with a wink. "Now go get that man before he slips away and is lost to you forever."

With that directive, she closed her lids again. Romantic pep-talk done.

Exhaustion washed over Cher in a tsunami. She placed her hands on her thighs and pushed to standing. When she crossed to the brother and sister who sat deep in a hushed conversation, they ceased speaking. Both looked up at her and for the first time, she noted the resemblance. Both shared the dark brows and hair with a pronounced widow's peak, the straight nose, and the blue eyes.

She unbuttoned her overalls and allowed the plackets to fall until the puffy protective layer hung by the snaps at her hips. "I'm going to try to get a bit of sleep while I can. That ride took a lot out of me."

Ethan stood and placed his hands on her shoulders. "Are you okay? Can we do anything?"

Weariness settled over her, pulling her down, like she'd be a puddle on the floor if she didn't get to a soft, flat surface soon. "Wake me if it sounds like they're trying to break through."

The concern in his gaze morphed to stony determination. "Will do."

She dragged her feet across the short space, past the stocks of canned provisions stacked on their shelves, and over to the bed. She unsnapped her overalls at the hip, unlaced her boots and pulled the heavy and now quite warm snowsuit from her. Each movement sapped more of her waning strength. With a last burst of effort, she swung her legs up onto the lower bunk across from her grandma and lay her head on the pillow.

What a damn day...

A rough shove rocked her shoulder.

*What...?*

"Cher. Wake up. There's something going on outside." A male voice.

Ethan. Her heart fluttered. She lifted her lids and found a pair of beautiful eyes, the color of a crisp, New Mexico spring sky. Ethan, already shifted, knelt beside her.

Disoriented and shaking, she pushed to sitting and ran a hand through her hair until she reached the elastic band. Her mouth seemed packed with cotton and her eyes gritty under the lids. When she spoke, her words emerged more like a croak. "What's going on?"

"Sounds like help has arrived, and all hell is breaking loose outside."

While he spoke, the muffled sounds of battle met her ears, driving away her sleep fog. She shoved her feet in her boots and tied the laces. "Where's my gun?"

He handed her the weapon with its slide locked back, along with a full magazine and an extra round. "I reloaded for you while you slept."

Ethan had the other gun in his hand, apparently ready to

fight. She dropped her gaze as she forced the lump in her throat down. Business. She needed to get back to business. She glanced across the aisle. Her grandmother still slept.

"Terri can take my place behind the provisions, like Grandma. The stacks of cans might help lessen a round's effectiveness, especially if she lays against the wall. Let's tip the table. It's metal and about the only cover we'll have if they find where we are and break through."

He nodded. "You take the table. I'll take the corner along the wall."

Ah ha. He'd have no cover, but he'd have the element of surprise.

"Good idea."

He turned the heavy table so the top faced the door, and she crouched behind, while Terri took up her position behind the provisions.

Tension crowded on Cher's shoulders as the moments ticked by. Would the house be there once the fighting ended? The shouts outside the safe room grew louder, the explosions and gunshots heavier.

Then silence.

Five taps on the rock sounded salvation's chimes.

Cher rose, her knees stiff from holding the crouched position for several minutes. She crossed to the wall. With a pause, she gathered her roiling emotions—relief NACS arrived, joy her grandmother would be safe, fear for Ethan's and his sister's impending journey back to Enchanted Rock, and sadness she may never see him again. Finally, she squeaked out, "Ro?"

"The one and only." Ro's muffled voice had never sounded so welcome. "You guys okay in there?"

Relief sagged Cher's shoulders, and she reached for the moonstone pendant to open the door. Ethan appeared at her side. Wait. He had a gun and was a wanted gargoyle. "Yep. Gimme a minute."

"Okay..." Ro's drawn out word indicated she didn't understand why she wasn't let in immediately, but would stay put.

Cher turned to Ethan and held out a hand. Since her lion shifter friend's hearing was too good, she whispered, "I'll need that. They might take it the wrong way."

Without a word, he offered the pistol to her, grip first. He showed no hesitation. As if he trusted her and would give no resistance.

Cher's gaze met his, and her heart cracked. This was a good man who may have made the only decision he could. One who understood the value of family and was willing to own up to his responsibilities. She didn't meet many of those suspect-type of people in her line of work.

At least if she had to have a mate she couldn't have, he was honorable. His stern face swam in her vision. A bare whisper escaped her mouth. "I'm sorry."

"Me too." His low voice rumbled only for her ears.

She checked the safety on the weapon he handed her, then tucked the pistol into her jean's back waistband. With her free hand moving in what felt like slo-mo, she pulled the charm and applied the moonstone to the lock mechanism, allowing NAC Security into her safe room.

And pushed Ethan from her heart.

# CHAPTER 12

"Come on, you." Ro's voice drifted from over Cher's shoulder. "Mingo's for one drink. You've been hiding from me for two weeks now."

Cher swung around in her chair to find her friend in her office. Ro's hands were propped on her hips, and she glared with the fierceness of a lioness. While Cher recognized the pose, she'd never been the recipient before. Yet, for all her friend's intensity, Cher felt a weariness, not intimidation.

She rubbed her forehead where an ache had begun to throb over one eye. "I'm on deadline. How about next week?"

"Nope," Ro stepped forward and hauled Cher up by her arms. "We're going to Mingo's. It's seven-thirty, and I know you came in early. Bet you've been here since six."

Of course she had. Because she hadn't been able to sleep. Night after sleepless night she tossed, thumped her pillow, stared at the ceiling. During those times when she *had* been able to close her eyes, the image of Ethan being led away in handcuffs filled her dreams. With his back stiff and purposeful, he'd glanced over his shoulder after Ro put the cuffs on him.

The promise in his gaze seared into Cher's memory, a reminder of something she could never have.

"I'm just busy right now." Despite the tepid protest, she snagged her purse. Her friend had a point. Cher needed to get back to a regular schedule of work and sleep. And food.

She and Ro ducked out a side exit. Cher snuck a glance up at her friend. The lion shifter radiated good health and happiness. Being in love wasn't hurting her either. Her dark, glowing skin and the lightness in her step seemed at odds with the lack of sleep she should be getting with her mate, Nash, after their recent reunion.

"You're looking a bit tired." Ro's gaze slid to the corner of her eye. "Have you had trouble sleeping lately?"

"Why would you think that?" Stupid question. She looked like hell's dumpster.

Ro's laugh carried the suggestion of a disbelieving snort. "Because the bags under your eyes have bags, and you look like you've dropped ten pounds. It's that Ethan guy, isn't it?"

How could Cher admit she may have fallen for a suspect? She remained mute, trying to think of reasons to invalidate her feelings, but she couldn't lie to others, and she wouldn't lie to herself.

Ro's long strides ate up the short distance to Enchanted Rock's most popular bar, Mingo's. On a Tuesday after happy hour, the bar had a good amount of empty spaces. Ro chose a tall table in a back corner. The distance from others and the music blaring in from the dance club area next door should be enough to cover any conversation from prying paranormal hearing.

The prompt server asked for their drink order. Ro requested a red wine.

Cher didn't have the desire for alcohol right now. Besides,

just about everything made her stomach queasy. She chose a ginger ale.

"Ginger ale?" Ro's leonine gaze narrowed and she sat back, crossing her arms. "What is going on?"

"I'm just busy."

Ro's predator half snatched that short, pathetic sentence and chowed down. "Since when did you start lying to me?"

Guilt wallowed in Cher's gut and mixed with the acid left there due to the lack of food. The combo felt like it ate through her stomach's lining and continued lower. Fortunately, the server arrived with the drinks, and Cher took a healthy swallow to settle her innards.

She put the glass down carefully in the center of the cocktail napkin. While her words hadn't exactly been a lie—the crime business never seemed to slow down—her friend deserved the truth.

"It's so weird, Ro. Like I've betrayed my own family by turning him in. I understand why he did what he did—family is the most important thing to me, you know that." She lifted her shoulders, hating the misery in her tone. "I'm just so confused right now about what I should do."

"Don't be. Ethan Porter? You saved his life. And that no-good-sister of his too." Ro's mouth twisted with her words while she twirled the wine glass's stem between her fingers. "Without you, they'd have been tiny bits floating in the Gulf or buried in the desert or zapped into the hereafter. He should be happy to be alive, not causing you heartburn."

Ha. If Ro only knew. But she should. No secrets between them. "I'm his mate."

Ro stilled. "You're his mate?"

Cher nodded and shifted her focus to the bubbles in her soda's glass. Ro would surely explode, either with laughter or derision, neither of which Cher could anticipate.

"Gargoyles have a mate?"

The calm question shocked Cher, and she raised her gaze to her friend, who studied her with narrowed lids. Since the small number of gargoyles who escaped their masters' control mainly kept to themselves, many didn't know their secrets. "When the Unseelie created them for their army, they literally used the essence of a shifter—strong and fast healing. One of the aspects that transferred over was a weaker form of mating. No...urges or despondency when they are denied their chosen, just a vague sense of incompleteness, or that's what I've been told."

*And exactly how I feel right now.*

Ro's nostrils flared, and she set her empty glass down with a snap. "Doesn't matter. He may have a mate, but you're an HP. You don't feel the mating call."

"Yeah, well..." Cher picked small pieces from the edge of the damp napkin under her soda.

Ro leaned forward, her eyes glittering slits. "Well what?"

"I don't know. He's a decent guy who made a wrong choice because he promised his father to take care of Terri. Dumb to run like that, but if she wouldn't turn herself in, can you blame him?" Cher rolled her eyes with a sad head shake. "Can you imagine the pain he'd feel to break his promise? It wouldn't go away until he fulfilled his oath. And if she went to jail?"

For a moment, Cher thought her friend would scoff or blow off the danger. Instead, Ro flopped back against her chair and crossed her arms. "The jailhouse grapevine would put out the bounty, and she'd be dead within the week. Not that I'd be all that mad."

"Ro!"

"Okay, okay, but she's a pain in the ass. You have to admit

that." She held up a hand and lifted her chin to someone over Cher's shoulder, probably the server.

Cher couldn't disagree. "Terri was a total pain in the ass, though I think she may have learned her lesson with this one. And she doesn't deserve death."

"Umm." Ro studied her glass. "If she learned her lesson, she may be able to avoid that sure death sentence."

Avoid? How… Cher fit the puzzle pieces together from Ro's cryptic remark. "They're going to work her?"

Ro's shoulders stiffened, then the tension released as quickly and she grimaced. "Should've known better than to say something to you. You're too quick. They want to know who's managing to defeat our oath spells."

"Well, I hope she can get a new start. But it still leaves her brother hanging out there as a target to pull her out of hiding." The idea he'd still be in danger grated. Unless… "They'll kill her off to give her the new start."

Ro smirked with Cher's finger quotes around the word 'kill'. She looped an arm over the back of her chair. "You shouldn't surprise me, Cher Velasco. Definitely too quick." She paused while the server delivered the new drinks, then leaned her folded arms on the table. "But enough about Terri Porter. You're attracted to her brother. Why?"

Cher had two weeks to try to figure it out, so the answers were pretty easy. "He's a family guy. He holds his promises."

"Only because he has to. He's a gargoyle." Ro half-snorted a laugh.

"True." Cher took a sip of ginger ale to settle her stomach, because murder hornets seemed to buzz around inside. Ro wasn't an attack-my-friend-and-I'll-forgive-you kind of shifter. Then again, Cher hadn't been very forgiving of Ro's mate when he supposedly betrayed her either.

Ro tapped the table with her index finger. "You should've had charges filed against him."

Cher set her glass carefully on the shredded napkin and held up a supplicating hand. "He did what he thought was right at the time. I don't blame him for that. He let me go almost immediately, Ro. And Director Constantin has enough charges stacked on him for helping his sister. He'll be in jail for some time."

The lion shifter's mouth pursed, obviously not convinced. Then her gaze narrowed over Cher's shoulder. "In jail, eh?"

The sharp tone cut through Cher's misery. She whipped her head around in the direction of her friend's stare.

Ethan cut through the tables toward her.

Her heart crashed against her ribs, then began flopping around like a caged bat. How?

A lion's growl rumbled behind her, but Cher couldn't tear her gaze away from the gargoyle approaching her. The promise glowing there transfixed her. "Stop, Ro. It'll be okay."

"Sure it will." Ro's chair scraped against the granite floor.

Ethan's gaze had connected with hers, and he appeared to not even see Ro, the agent who'd arrested him two weeks ago. "Can we talk?" he asked, his tone low and urgent.

From Cher's periphery, Ro came to stand at Cher's shoulder. "No. You need to leave my friend alone. She doesn't need a—"

"Please, Ro." Cher ripped her gaze from his and returned her focus to her friend, who appeared ready as a mamma lion to defend a cub. 'Please,' Cher mouthed.

Ro's jaw tightened, "I don't like it." Nevertheless, she spun and stalked away.

Over Ethan's shoulder, Cher tracked her friend to the other side of the bar. Far away enough to not overhear, but close enough to watch the two of them. The lion shifter already had her mobile phone to her ear, no doubt calling legal to learn why Ethan walked free.

The question deserved an answer. She swiveled her attention back to him. "Why were you released?"

His gaze slid over his shoulder to the rest of the bar. "It's a long story and not for public consumption. Can we take a walk?"

Though her heart wanted to say 'yes,' her practical, NACS side said 'stay put.' She trusted him, but... "No. We can do this right here. No one can overhear us over the music if we're quiet."

He took the stool at a ninety-degree angle with his back to the crowd. "The charges were dropped."

"Dropped?" The word didn't want to register. She hadn't allowed herself to hope. Her heart and will would have been crushed when he went to prison.

He nodded and he looked down at his hands folded on the table's top. "Terri's dead."

"Dead, huh?" She leaned in and whispered just loud enough for him to hear over the blare from the speakers. "They're allowing her to work it off, huh?"

His lids lifted, and he sucked a swift breath. "How'd you guess?"

She tapped her temple. "I put puzzle pieces together for a living, remember? But that doesn't completely explain why you're off the hook. Either she has A-plus information or you helped the investigators too."

A slow, appreciative grin spread across his handsome visage. "Both. I gave them everything I knew about the Sunda Komodo family. I think they're close to wrapping up that investigation."

The knowledge he put himself further in harm's way sliced at her heart. "Will you have to testify?"

"Maybe." He grimaced and sat straighter as if facing a foul potion.

The slice became a canyon in her chest and she moved her hand to cover one of his, warm and real after two weeks of dream Ethan. The contact soothed her soul while his actions raised her fear. "But that's so dangerous. They'll come after you."

He nodded, his face as serious as solemn an ancient fae grave. "No more dangerous than what you did to save me and Terri." He pursed his lips, then said, "These two weeks have been an eye-opener, Cher. I know what I did was wrong, but I also would have to do it again because of Terri and her poor choices. I can't thank you enough. You seemed to get through to her what I couldn't. I'm just sorry I put you and your grandmother in danger. How is she?"

His question buoyed her. "She's fine. She knew you and Terri weren't husband and wife, you know," Cher almost confided her grandmother thought he was the 'one,' but she inexplicably stopped short.

"I don't think I'm cut out for a life of deception. At least you taught me that." With his other hand he turned his warm, strong palms to cup hers with what seemed almost reverence. "Thank you, Cher Velasco. Thank you for everything. I know you aren't able to take a chance on me because of my history. I accept that now."

His sad, resigned smile bombarded her with confusing emotions, which formed a hot, scorching ball in her throat.

Before she could swallow, he rose. "Take care of yourself and your grandmother."

*Wait, what's happening?* A firmer voice immediately said, *You know this is the best thing.* No sound would come through her throat, and none of her limbs seemed to be working.

All she could was watch the one man she might've been able to love walk away.

The hard slam of a door echoed in her head, as final as the one in Enchanted Rock's jail.

# CHAPTER 13

E than swooped down and landed at the forest's edge about half a mile from the ranch house. At dusk's last gasp, he had little fear of being seen at this distance, despite the barren trees.

Cher helped him keep his word to his sister. In return, he vowed he'd watch over her grandmother. Maybe he hadn't told Cher about his promise specifically, but he would hold to the promise he made to himself.

No bright lights shone from where he knew the kitchen and living area to be.

They should be on already.

The change in routine concerned him. While he'd circled high above monitoring the property with his enhanced gargoyle vision, the nurse's vehicle remained parked in front. Maybe the power had gone out? No. The security light at the barn several hundred yards from the house glowed a bright pink.

Uneasiness coated his gut like rancid oil. Because the lights failed to turn on like they had for the past three weeks he'd watched over Ms. Two-Birds?

Yes.

Agent Nlongo told him they suspected mobster Griffith Jenkins for the attack over a month ago. Had the criminal sent more assassins in retaliation? An approaching vehicle caught his ear and he tensed. Seconds later, a black SUV raced up the drive, bouncing and veering on the dirt path still partially covered in snow.

Would this be a friend or foe? At that speed, the driver wouldn't be able to take their eyes from the road, so he launched, using his wings to pull him up, up, gaining speed and distance like a rocket. Then he tucked his wings back and hurtled back to earth, back to the unknown SUV which skidded to a halt right in front of the door. The driver exited.

Cher.

His heart's hard thump should've cracked his granite skin. Why was she here? And why was she driving like a drunk banshee?

Ethan pulled up only about a hundred yards from the back of the vehicle, extending his wings in an effort not to reveal himself. His muscles vibrated with the strain, but he swooped away silently.

"Come out here you cowardly motherfucker!"

Was she shouting at him? He banked over the barn a couple of hundred yards away.

But she didn't focus in his direction. She stood short of the front door, speaking to the house.

Someone inside? Who else other than Cher's grandmother and the woman's nurse could be in there? He hadn't missed anyone going in.

Cher said something he couldn't quite catch, so he dropped a couple hundred feet to where the wind wasn't as fierce. He hovered on silent wings in the dark sky. Fear and fury tore at him that he may have missed something—but what?

"...I'm here. What do you want?" She'd put one fist on her hip.

"I want *you*, of course."

Ethan almost froze with the sibilant hiss on the last word. He knew that male voice.

Karil Sunda, the very Komodo Shifter who had accepted the money from Terri to pay off Father's debts.

Stunned, Ethan dropped then remembered to beat his wings. Why here? And how? And why? They were paid. They'd been *paid*.

Dammit. His testimony.

Guilt slithered though him. He'd failed Cher and her grandmother.

He shoved aside the horror spiraling within him. The two must get to safety.

How did the shifter get in? *Think!*

The only thing which made sense would be if Sunda took a New ID potion to resemble the nurse. No one else had gone in or out of the house. Fear slithered down his spine. The Komodo mobster would kill both Cher and her grandmother. No witnesses was their specialty.

"Dunno why you want me," Cher responded. "I've never done anything to you."

"No, you haven't, but you'll be a nice bait for a gargoyle."

Ethan's blood froze in his veins with the confirmation. No. He was supposed to be watching over Ms. Two-Birds, and he'd done a shit job.

"Gargoyle? I only know one. Dr. Schofield in the Medical Examiner's office."

Ethan blessed her for buying any amount of time. How could he get to the damn shifter? One way only.

"Come now, Ms. Velasco. You know one more. A little birdie told me he might be sweet on you." Sunda's voice, though amiable, held a dose of undeniable menace.

Not much time left. He couldn't let her be taken. Bad enough he might've allowed Ms. Two-Birds to be killed.

Once again he folded back his wings and dove.

"Another? You mean Ethan Porter? The NACS suspect?" She laughed, scathing scorn in her tone.

Surely she was acting. Yes. She had to be. *Keep him occupied.* Ethan's trajectory aimed him at the earth next to the front of the house. At the very last moment, he snapped his wings and zipped through the side of the porch.

Sunda turned toward him with a gun in his hand. His eyes widened. But that was a mere blip of recognition before Ethan slammed into him, wrapping his arms around the nurse who wasn't the nurse. As he tumbled with the other body, Cher screamed.

Before Ethan stopped rolling, the nurse morphed into a giant Komodo dragon. The creature writhed, and its dry, scaled skin felt slick and slippery in his arms. Long claws scraped, but didn't break, Ethan's skin.

"Get inside to your grandmother!"

Ethan couldn't turn to see if she complied with his directive. With an evil hiss, Sunda lunged with his mouth and latched onto Ethan's arm. The deadly teeth ground into Ethan's granite flesh. With his free hand, he punched the Komodo directly in the orange, vertically-slitted eye. Victory shot though him when the eye popped with a wet squish.

Sunda released his arm with a gurgle and slapped a foot to his face. He flailed wildly with his heavy tail, easily the same length as the giant lizard himself, as well as with the long talons of his free foot. His open-mouthed hiss warned Ethan to back off.

Not a chance. If he let the dragon go, he'd just try again. No way could Ethan let the shifter get to the two females.

Ethan feinted toward the side with the bad eye, then ducked under the Komodo's flashing claws, which skittered down his back and caught his wings. One ripped. Shards of agony spiraled through him, but he kept going to his target.

The reptile's neck.

He sank his fangs deep. Vaguely he heard the shifter's scream. *Keep going.* Ethan tore, bit again. *Keep going!* He reached for the Komodo's lower jaw, pushed it up to make the neck even more vulnerable. More bites. He became a chomping machine, chewing through the Komodo dragon to defeat him. He spit the pieces of flesh from his mouth. The tail crashed into his ankles, but he managed to stay upright. He pushed up more on the jaw. Cher must be safe. Another bite.

Bone.

With both of his hands, he grasped the reptile's upper jaw, using the curved teeth as a way for his blood-slicked fingers to gain traction, pushing the head back until he exposed the spinal column. With a mighty heave, he pulled the head back.

Snap.

He tore the head from the rest of the flesh and tossed it into the yard. Even if he left the head attached by just skin, the shifter could regenerate.

Grim satisfaction curled Ethan's fists and he wanted to punch them in the air, he'd won.

The enormous reptile body ceased moving and sagged into Ethan. He pushed it away and let the headless reptilian behemoth collapse to the wooden porch's floorboards. All thoughts of victory fled and Ethan leaned his hands on his thighs, every muscle shaking. For a moment, all he could do was breathe as his heart thundered like a stampeding herd in his ears. Then he focused on the body before him.

He'd killed someone.

By chewing through their neck.

Instead of horror, the calm knowledge of his deed filled his mind. The someone he killed had threatened his mate. He'd saved her.

"Ethan?"

The voice seemed to come from far away, maybe from as far as the fae realm itself.

Everything became an effort. Breathing. Hearing. Seeing. He pushed hard from his thighs and struggled to stand upright. He staggered to the side, hitting his hip hard against the railing, shattering the wood, and falling on his side into the snow piled up against the footings.

He landed with a grunt. Snow was harder than he realized. And surprisingly cold. He tried to push up, but for some reason his arms wouldn't do his bidding.

A shadow grew in his vision, and Cher's form came into focus. She had a device with an antenna held to her mouth.

"Ro, red, red, red. Get the team in here now. Ethan's hurt."

"The team?" He hated how his words sounded slurred and low. What was wrong with him? He'd just torn apart a Komodo dragon shifter. He should be glorying, roaring in victory. Instead, he could barely move, barely speak. Had he been injured when—

The pain from his wings hit him with brutal intensity, an all-consuming fire which threatened his very sanity. He tried to glance over his shoulder, but the effort became too much. Darkness gathered at the edges of his vision.

"Shh." Cher's soft hand stroked his cheek "Don't move. Help is on its way."

With his mate's assurance, Ethan closed his eyes and sank into the blackness.

# CHAPTER 14

C her stared at Ethan where he lay on her bed facedown, in deference to his healing wings. Best to leave him that way, the med team had said. One of the wings had hung on by a shred of skin, while the other had been dislocated in the fight with the Komodo. Both sustained substantial damage—broken bones and shredded skin. The technician tranquilized him, along with giving him a variety of healing potions.

For what had to be the hundredth time, she forced herself to stay in the chair rather than get up and pace. The NACS team surveyed the crime scene for several hours, interviewing Cher and her grandmother, who was mercifully unharmed, and even got a warrant to read Ethan's memories. And fortunately, they found the nurse, hurt, but alive, and worked to bring her back to full strength.

Most importantly, NACS took away the Komodo piece of shit—pieces of shit—in her grandmother's front yard.

Ro appeared in the doorway to Cher's bedroom. With her gaze inscrutable, she said, "We're taking off now."

"Charges?" The roiling acid in Cher's stomach bubbled more with Ro's carefully guarded expression.

"No. Seems he acted in defense of you and your grand-mother. He had no idea we were backing you up." The lion shifter started to turn toward the hallway, then reversed her course. "I think I may have misjudged him. He's been here for the last couple of weeks watching over your grandmother. Maybe he's not the gargoyle I thought he was."

He'd been watching over her grandmother since he left her? Her stomach seemed to settle a little with both pieces of news and the fact Ro had changed her mind about him. "Thanks."

Ethan wouldn't be charged. But the potential allegations were only a part of her anxiety. What to do with her confused feelings for this gargoyle? Ro had all but given her the thumbs up.

Cher's thoughts tumbled over each other.

With Ro's departure, the bustling sounds and voices in the house faded away. A *click-slide-click-slide* sounded from the hall-way, and Cher focused her attention on her grandmother, who carefully rounded the jamb.

"Mija. You get some dinner. I left your plate on the counter. I can watch him."

The thought of food, however delicious, soured her stomach once more. "Thanks, Abuelita. I'll come later."

The old woman clucked her tongue. "He's going to wonder when you turned into skin and bones."

"Ha." She patted her waistline in an attempt to bamboozle her grandmother. "Since when have I not eaten?"

"Never. That's why I'm worried." Her gaze softened behind her thick lenses, and she gathered Cher's hands into hers. "Give him a chance. For me?"

Momentarily, Cher's world spun on its axis. The older woman released her hands and the *click-slide* faded away. Should Cher heed her grandma? She'd always believed if she found a male, he'd be upstanding, and never been in trouble. But this one. He'd been nothing but in trouble since she met him.

But never officially proven to be trouble…

He'd been absolutely kind. Well, except for the kidnapping thing, but he relented quickly when he found out she feared for her grandmother.

He tried to protect his sister. And now her abuela.

Could she give him a chance?

"You don't have to, you know."

She bolted out of her chair with Ethan's mumbled words and stopped beside the bed. His left eye glowed its brilliant paranormal blue. A shyness struck her, totally foreign and stealing her confidence. "You're awake."

*Duh. Of course he's awake.*

He moved his arms under the pillow to cradle his cheek in them. After a slight turn toward his back, his expression twisted and air hissed through his fangs.

"Don't move." She thrust out a hand to stop him and came into contact with his warm, silky skin. Her neurons fired with the contact, scrambling all cognition, shredding any resistance.

She yanked her fingers away, which allowed thought once more beyond her silly inability to summon coherent thought. "Sunda almost tore off one of your wings. The med team said since you had a Cure Now in the last two months, it would be best not to have another. Apparently, there's a two-per-year restriction on those. So, that's why you're not totally healed, and why you're still in gargoyle form. They thought you would heal better that way…" Cher's babbling words trailed off, and her face turned to fire.

The corner of his eye crinkled in time with the curl of his lips. "Any other medical things I need to know?"

"No. Uh, well, no." She swung away and placed her hands

to her blazing cheeks. Who was this girl who couldn't control herself around a male? She jammed her hands back into her jeans pockets and turned back to him. "Not medical at least. I came today with an NACS backup team."

He stiffened with a grimace, so she hastily continued, "They said it appeared you were defending me and my grandmother, so they were going to recommend no charges be filed."

He released a heavy breath. "That's sounds good."

"And they did a search warrant on your thoughts."

"They read my mind?" His brows slammed together.

Though guilt niggled at her for the violation of his personal thoughts, if it had kept him out of trouble, she had zero regrets. "Only for the reason why you were here and the intent of your attack on Sunda. Thank you for being here and protecting my grandmother. I couldn't get away from work, so I'd paid for a couple of wards and spells, but in the end, the bad guys figured out a way, didn't they?"

"You had a team to help you, so I wasn't really needed." His dismissal of his own actions brought tears to her eyes. He could've died.

She rushed back to the bed. "No, Ethan, you were definitely needed. I can't thank you enough."

His glowing cerulean blue eye closed and his tone grew weary. "No thanks needed. You saved my ass and my sister's. Don't listen to your grandmother because you think you owe me some sort of debt."

"Isn't that what you did here, because you felt you owed me a debt?"

"No."

"Then why…" The reason might as well have been a round-house to her head. Oh hell. "She's family."

No response.

How could she not at least say 'maybe' to this male? One who took family as seriously as she, one who would treat her abuela as his own, one who was kind...well, until he bit and ripped the Komodo dragon shifter's head clean off. Instead of revulsion, satisfaction swelled within her.

He protected his own.

Cher perched on the edge of the double bed, if only because he took up almost the entirety. She folded her hands in her lap. "What else can I say, Ethan, other than—"

"I understand you can't be in a relationship with someone who's been a suspect in a crime." The defeat in his tone nearly tore her heart in two.

She laid a hand on his shoulder, marveling how the skin underneath her palm remained warm and pliant despite its flecked-granite appearance. She said, her voice soft, "You shouldn't interrupt someone, you know."

His one visible eye cracked open. "Don't mess with me, Cher."

"I'm not. I had a long-standing mantra that I didn't make life decisions based on a guy. And quitting my job qualified as a life-decision." She stared at the Duran Duran poster still hanging on her wall. Time to be an adult.

"Quitting your job? Why would you do that?" His words emerged guarded, as if her reply could shatter his entire world.

"For you."

He shifted, rolling to one shoulder with a wince. "Not for me."

"Yep."

"You quit your job?"

"Nope. I didn't have to."

"Because..."

"You aren't a felon, and all charges have been dropped." She shifted to face him and took his hand in hers, tracing the tendons with her thumb. "I was so shocked when you found me in Mingo's."

The dull blue of his eyes blazed. "Then if I'm not charged and I'm not a felon, does that mean…?'

"It means 'maybe,' Ethan. We have a lot of core values in common, but what if I can't stand that you leave socks on the floor?"

He turned over his hand, linking his fingers with hers. "No socks on the floor. Ever. I'll make sure it's a 'yes.'"

"But what if we don't—"

"No what ifs." He held up a hand. "And no more interruptions. May I kiss you? At least we can figure out if we're compatible in that way."

Kissing. Above all else she wanted to kiss him right now. Would it be as good as those in her dreams? She must know.

Carefully, she leaned down, fitting her lips to his, exploring, seeking.

Her dreams had gotten the sensations all wrong. She deepened their contact, sweeping in with her tongue to dance with his. He didn't just taste good. He tasted of chocolate and sin and a desire which may never fade.

She pulled away, her heart hammering against her ribs and her chest rising and falling too rapidly. She already missed the contact. Her gaze tangled with his and the corners of his lips curled in a most self-satisfied grin.

"What do you think? Are we compatible in that way?"

"Maybe, Ethan. Maybe."

## A Note from Amanda Reid

Hello! Just a short message to say I hope you enjoyed this book and to ask if you would leave a review of *The Gargoyle Dilemma*? We independently published authors need your input, as do other readers to find the stories they want to read. It can be as simple or as detailed as you like. And thank you in advance!

Also, check out my website for an awesome *FREE* novella, *The Puma's Second Chance*, available when you sign up for my newsletter, which will also feature promos, insights into my little writing world (its okay—y'all know me here!), and other awesome stuff. Check out www.amandareidauthor.com for more details.

*Until we read again,*
*Amanda*

PS—Turn the page for my next exciting Enchanted Rock Immortals novella, *The Demon's Choice*!

# The Demon's Choice
## An Enchanted Rock Immortals Novella
## by Amanda Reid

Human paranormal Terri Porter did a monumentally stupid thing—she tried to free her brother from loan sharks by cheating other underworld families. Now she must stay alive long enough for redemption.

Beyond Terri's razor-sharp sarcasm, she has zero helpful skills to protect herself until she can testify in an Enchanted Rock court against a mage and earn her freedom. Enter the infuriating, arrogant Berith, a demon and North American Council Security officer who not only possesses the skills she needs to keep her safe, but also makes her body sing with desire and yearn for a love she can never have.

How could he have pissed off the Fates this much? Berith Lequare considers rejecting the assignment to keep Terri alive —after all, she'd betrayed her oath and put a coworker's life at risk. But if there's one thing this demon will do, it's his duty, even when it raises specters of a past devastation...even when his entire being craves to taste Terri's blood as he sinks himself deep into her beautiful body.

In a paranormal world where nothing is guaranteed, blood is a commodity, and threats lay around every corner, can Terri and Berith stay alive long enough to defeat the ghosts of their pasts and find true love?

***The Demon's Choice*** is available in ebook and paperback, exclusively through Kindle and Kindle Unlimited!

# ABOUT THE AUTHOR

Amanda Reid authors not only Enchanted Rock Immortals urban fantasy romance novellas, but also the Flannigan Sisters Psychic Mysteries, a paranormal cozy mystery series.

Since she was young, she's been a lover of mystery, sci-fi, and paranormal genres. Amanda found her first romance book in her aunt's closet around thirteen years of age and quickly decided it needed to be added to her repertoire.

Beyond writing, Amanda was a career Army brat and lived in exotic locations like Tehran, Iran and DeRidder, Louisiana as a child. She dreamed of a career in the State Department, but ended up as a federal agent. For 24 years Amanda investigated murders, fraud, identity theft, drug trafficking and many other crimes before her retirement. As you can imagine, it's given her a wealth of inspiration for her mystery and urban fantasy stories.

She currently lives in Texas with her husband and two gonzo Australian Shepherds. Click on the icons below to catch up with her on Facebook, Twitter or Instagram. You can sign up for upcoming releases and promos at amandareidauthor.com.

Made in the USA
Columbia, SC
12 November 2024

46295082R00076